The Unpublishables

By Noah Goats

*I know I was writing stories when I was five. I don't know
what I did before that. Just loafed I suppose.*

P.G. Wodehouse

Chapter 1

I'll admit that what I'm about to say isn't based on any kind of physical evidence, eye witness account, circumstantial evidence, or even the drunken ramblings of the neighborhood conspiracy theorist, but I think you'll agree that we live in a country that has been caught in the grip of a bizarre mass mental illness, and the theory I am about to propound would go a long way towards explaining it.

Several years ago, a bioengineered virus escaped from a top-secret military research facility in North Dakota, or someplace equally bleak. This virus was created by the Pentagon to deal with the Russians. We can pretend as much as we want that Muslim extremists or the Chinese are our most dangerous national enemies, but I was born before the Berlin Wall fell and I know better. The Russians were the villains of my childhood, the bad guys in Rocky IV, Red Dawn, and the 1988 Olympics. For me they will always be the sentimental enemy.

I imagine the plan looked something like this: If the CIA ever discovered that the Russians were about to launch World War III, the United States would immediately load a weaponized version of the virus onto a fleet of SR-71 Blackbirds retrofitted with crop dusting equipment. These supersonic crop dusters would spray the pathogen over Moscow, St. Petersburg, and whatever other cities the Russians might have. Overnight, the virus would remove the danger of Russian aggression because the purpose of this pathogen was to infect the brain with a severe form of graphomania: an insatiable drive to write novels. Once all those frosted Slavs caught the disease, they would lose any sense of military aggression, spending all their time writing interminable epics. Once a Russian gets writing he doesn't stop until his book can be used as a stepping stool thick enough to allow Danny DeVito to reach the cereal on the highest shelf at the grocery store. They would be trapped behind a wall of their own words.

Unfortunately, the weaponized disease somehow leaked from the top secret facility and spread from person to person all across this country, and now every single American has been swept away by a mania for novel writing. Pay attention to the world around you. Go to the nearest coffee shop and look at all those glowing laptops. Is that normal? Mention fiction to a friend and wait for him to launch the plot of his own thriller at you. Every man thinks he has a novel in him, and now the novels are trying to get out.

No disease has a kill rate of a hundred percent and a portion of the population will always be immune. Even the bubonic plague didn't kill everybody. In the case of this specific man-made virus, it appears that I am the only person with an immune system capable of fighting it off. I am the only man left, as far as I can see, who doesn't want to write a novel. I am the Omega Man.

Again, I can't prove any of this. In fact, now that I read it, this story about a novel writing virus seems to be exactly the sort of plot device that might occur to someone who wants to write fiction. But I don't want to write fiction. I'm just trying to make sense of the world.

"What's your novel about?" she asked, just like I knew she would.

I had seen her walk into the bar about 37 seconds before she popped that worn out old question. I had watched her glide across the room with that question already puckered on her lips. She was worth watching, all blond and bouncy. She caught me looking at her and I immediately turned away

2

and became absorbed in my drink. Maybe she would read my body language for the message it was clearly signaling: DON'T TALK TO ME. This was a message that radiated out of me at a low level at all times; I now merely attempted to amplify it subtly.

She didn't read the signal. Women at her level of sexiness assume that every man wants to talk to them; so, she sat down on the stool right next to mine and gave me an opportunity to do just that. But I didn't rise to the fly. I let it float there and hoped it would drift away downstream. She cleared her throat pointedly and waited for me to look up at her. I pretended I hadn't heard. Finally, she asked the inevitable question, "What's your novel about?"

I hate this question. It's usually the first thought that erupts into my head in the morning. I wonder if it's because I'm always dreaming about being asked what my novel is about. I never remember my dreams, so I can't be sure, but I think the plague that is, "What's your novel about?" must follow me from my waking hours into my sleeping ones.

I ignored her, pretending that I hadn't heard. Maybe she would give up and go away.

She didn't go away. Instead, she repeated herself, "What's your novel about?"

"Oh. Uh. My novel?" As if I was surprised that she had asked me. "Well, you know, it's . . ."

Not only did I not have a novel, I didn't have a stack of legal pads full of the notes or the outline necessary to write one. I didn't even have a napkin tucked away in a drawer somewhere with an idea for a novel scribbled onto it. I had no ideas for any story of any kind. When I was walking around the city, or watching baseball, or spooning cereal into my mouth in the morning, a constant stream of thoughts flowed through my brain, but as soon as anyone asked me what my novel was about my stream would dry up; my mind would become blank. A void. A desert so sterile that there was not one tumbleweed to roll across it.

I couldn't tell her this of course. *Everyone* had a novel after all. I tried to think of an idea right there on the spot but, yet again, I drew a blank. An empty wordless page. I did own several hundred sheets of white printer paper, and I supposed that I could theoretically turn them into a novel, but, as yet, I had no idea how I might put letters and punctuation on those pages in a sequence that would make them more interesting and valuable than they were as blank paper.

So, I did what I had done so many times before when confronted with this question: I punted. "Why don't you tell me about your novel?" I asked. And she had the same reaction everyone had when they were asked to receive one of my punts: she looked confused and suspicious. She had, after all, just given me a chance to talk about my book. How could I pass up the opportunity to bring my characters to life for her, to blow her mind with my plot twists, to woo her with my love scenes that transmogrified themselves so tenderly into sex scenes?

At the same time, the only reason she had asked me about my book was to get me to let her tell me about hers. After studying my face for a moment, she gave in to the overpowering desire to share her work.

"Ok," she said, "you're going to like this! I'm still working on the rough draft, but I think it's going to be really good!" I was worried that she would pull out pages. A verbal synopsis of a book in progress is bad enough, but actual pages are almost always worse. Yes, they are more polished, more coherent, and better thought out, but they are also longer, and some kind of verbal synopsis is always connected to them anyway. Tell me about your book if you absolutely must, but please don't read an actual chapter to me.

"So, there's like this mystical planet called Algeron..." Oh no, it was a fantasy novel. The worst.

Her eyes were glowing as she began to tell her tale. I was glad that she didn't suffer from the shame that overcomes so many new writers who compulsively remind those hearing about the book in progress that it is, "just a rough draft," that, "needs a lot of work," and that at some vague time in the future it will not, "stink quite so much." Begging forgiveness for your book's awfulness is never a good way to start. It makes your listeners, your potential readers, uncomfortable. It turns you into an object of derision. It makes them pity you. It makes them feel embarrassed for you. But this girl wasn't that kind of writer at all. She had no doubt in her ability.

"On Algeron there are two types of people," she continued, "they are called the Floaters and the Sinkers." She paused here, giving me a moment to admire the Floaters and the Sinkers. I expressed a noncommittal sort of appreciation that she deemed, somewhat to my surprise, to be adequate.

"Both of these kinds of people live on the ground, but the Floaters are beautiful, and they can fly, and have wings, and are kind of like fairies. The Sinkers are ugly, and they can't fly, but they can swim. That's why they're called Sinkers. And I say they're ugly, but a few of them have swimmer's bodies and are actually pretty hot."

"Sounds interesting."

"Yeah, so there's this girl, and she's a Floater, and she is the hottest one of all." As she described the protagonist of her story it instantly became clear that she was only describing herself, idealized, with wings, but pretty much herself. Almost everyone's novel seemed to be about their

5

own sad selves, usually idealized or demonized versions. Few tried to use their imagination to step outside of themselves, to look into the souls of other people, to try to picture the life experiences of those who were different. It was usually just, "Here is a book about me, but I have big muscles and a sword in it."

"And this girl, her name is Carabella, that means 'beautiful face' in Italian, and she's a princess who lives on an island . . ." and then I zoned out for a while. I'd heard enough of this particular kind of thing to know what I was in for: a Disney type princess story with lots of hardcore sexual escapades.

So this Carabella meets a Sinker named Troy, he's the hot kind of Sinker with a swimmer's body, and they have about 15 pages worth of explicitly detailed and borderline violent sexual intercourse, and then, as soon as these are over, there are complications. Blah blah blah. The king forbids her to blah blah blah. Then there is a bunch of fighting, and finally my storyteller came to what she considered to be the great twist in her story, "So then, after all the laser gun fighting and the laser sword fighting, it turns out it's Carabella who kills her ex-boyfriend and saves Troy's life. Don't you think that's amazing? It's the girl who saves the boy in my novel!"

I had listened to all of this with an expression of interest bent unnaturally upon the features of my face. In our world of aspiring authors, everyone has learned to make this look of forced interest with its furrowed brow and flat lip of admiring concentration that can melt, when necessary, into a crooked grin and eyes twinkling with delight. But even though I had done this facial workout hundreds of times, it still exhausted me, and when she had at last finished telling me her tale I was relieved to allow my mouth to drift back to whatever shape is natural to it and to switch off the twinkle in my eye.

She paused for a moment. She was waiting for me to fill the silence with my praise, and when I didn't immediately respond she took the initiative back and asked me what I had thought of her story.

"Oh, it's very good," I assured her. It wasn't good. Obviously. But honest criticism is considered by most people to be a gross affront to good manners.

She paused again, waiting for more, and when I didn't give her more, she took the lead and began asking follow up questions.

"And what do you think was good about it?"

"The characters?"

"Is that all?"

"The plot. Really drives the whole thing."

She asked questions, and I gave her the shortest version possible of the acceptable answers for several minutes before I decided to ask her a question of my own. "Do you mind if I ask you a question about your book?" Of course she didn't. She could literally sit there and answer questions about her book until she became hoarse from talking, and even then she would probably continue answering by whatever method of sign language came to hand. (I recognize that there is a pun in that last sentence, and I beg you to overlook it. It was not intentional.) "What were your influences?"

"Oh, I had all kinds of influences, my aunt really inspired me to . . ."

"No, I mean, literary influences."

She looked confused, and maybe a little worried, as if she thought I was up to no good.

"Literary influences?"

"Yes, what books inspired you?"

"My novel," she declared haughtily, "is a wholly original work of art!"

"I'm sure it is, but I'm just curious about what kinds of books you like. What's your favorite book?"

"My own! The one I just told you about!"

"I mean, by someone else. The best book you've ever read by someone who was not you."

She looked irritated and off balanced by the question. "What does that have to do with anything?"

"Nothing, really. Consider it a change in topic. What books do you like to read? What are some of your favorite books?"

"My favorite books?" She sounded confused and clearly considered this change of topic unwelcome.

I realized that the conversation had become painful to her and awkward for both of us. I wished that I had just let her continue to talk about her novel, but it was too late for that. I tried to help her out, "Your book is a mix of fantasy and science fiction; do you like science fiction novels?"

"I like my book."

"Of course, but are there any other science fiction novels that you like?" I could see a sort of low-grade panic in her expression as she frantically searched her memory for any science fiction books she had ever read. Or at least heard about.

The silence was awkward, and the embarrassment was beginning to mount, so I tried to bail her out, "You know, like *The Hunger Games*?"

She narrowed her eyes as if she suspected a trap, "That was a book first?"

"Yes. It was a trilogy. Three books."

She undid the eye narrowing a little and allowed a smile to touch her lips, "Ugh, of course it was a series of books. I loved them! The whole thing with the archery and the flaming dress and the hunger. It was great!"

I decided that asking her anything else about any books other than her own would be cruel, and we lapsed into silence for a moment before she asked me a question that I wasn't prepared to answer. "How about you? What books inspired your novel?"

And then we were right back where we started. Back to my book. I realized I was just going to have to face the situation, "I, uh, I don't have a book. I don't write. I mean, I write, but not books. Just stuff for work. Memos. Spreadsheets. Emails."

She couldn't quite believe it. "You're not writing a novel?"

"No."

"A short one?"

"Nothing."

"Oh," she mumbled as her face stiffened, "I'm sorry." And then she got up and walked away, not knowing how to talk to a man who didn't have a novel to brag about. It's awkward, not being a novelist.

Chapter 2

To understand me and my problem, you have to understand where I come from.

I come from a quiet place.

It's a good town, with good schools, law abiding citizens, clean air, healthy children, and people of different races living together in perfect amity.

It's so boring.

It's a little prairie town in Kansas, called, I swear, Normalcy. I know. It sounds like I made the name of my hometown up; it's too on the nose to be real. But it is real. Remember, I don't write fiction. Check your Rand McNally Road Atlas for Kansas. You'll find it. It's there. The town plan is laid out on a perfect geometric grid. It is the flatness of the terrain that allows such geometrical perfection in the streets. People walk their dogs on these right-angled roads in the morning and they smile at each other. Folks say "hi" to one another when they pass on the even slabs of concrete that make up the sidewalk. Kids walk to school and it's so safe their parents don't need to walk with them. Some of them ride bikes with banana seats and tassels streaming from the handlebars. There are never any kidnappings in Normalcy.

I was a B student at Normalcy High.

I was on the football team, but mostly rode the bench.

My high school aptitude test said that the perfect job for me was "office work."

I have never been addicted to drugs. In fact, I have never even tried them. I do not smoke. I drink only in moderation.

I don't bet on cards, horses, rolls of the dice, or football. With the lone exception of the office March Madness pool, I am not a gambling man. I have never won the pool, by the way.

I went to a good college where I received a solid education in a practical field, and upon graduation I immediately found a job that pays well and placed me on the comfortable end of the middle class.

I was raised Episcopalian. And by that, I mean my parents said, "Episcopalian," when I asked them what our religion was. I had to ask because there was no church attendance that might have provided a clue. They were neither religious nor hostile to religion, and I have never put much thought into religion myself. I believe god is out there, and I hope for the best without worrying much about any possible details.

My parents loved me. They're still together. They love each other too.

I now live in San Francisco, which is the opposite of Normalcy in many ways, but Normalcy is rooted deep within me, and how could a person raised in such abnormal normality ever hope to write a novel? What would I write about? I don't have any life experiences. I know nothing about the shadows lurking in the human heart. I have never been poor. I have never been rich. Beyond the two colds I get every winter, I have never been sick. I have never had a loved one die. I am a thirty-seven-year-old man and every single one of my grandparents (all of whom are very sweet) is still alive.

I've had some girlfriends, but never a real rough breakup. All of my relationships have started out okay, and then entered a period of drifting apart, and then finally been terminated by mutual agreement when the two of us simply lost interest at more or less the same time.

In addition to my white, middle class, middle American upbringing, I can add my phlegmatic character. I sail through life on a perfectly even emotional keel. I'm not hot headed. I'm not particularly passionate. I don't fall into abysses of lust or love or hate or anger or . . . I'm just not sure that I feel things deeply enough. I have never, for as long as I can remember, ever cried. Not once. For joy or for sorrow. I'm sure I must have cried as a child, but if I did the event made no mental impression on me and I cannot remember it.

I think the better novelists probably have experience with the full range of normal human emotions. I have felt them all too, I guess, but not at extreme levels. There is simply no drama in me.

Both nature and nurture have made me entirely unfit to be a novelist.

And putting all that aside for one moment, I'm shocked that anyone, no matter their temperament, life experience, talent, or intelligence, dares to write a novel. There's just too much competition. Two hundred and fifty million able minded adults live in the United States, and as far as I can tell 249,999,999 of them are currently working on a novel. I suspect that more Americans are writing novels than have read one.

I hate to think of all the trees that have been murdered as a result of this novel writing mania, all the squirrels left homeless, all the birds with no branches left to chirp on. And why? To what end? What is this need that people have to express themselves through writing fiction? Can't they express themselves by talking to a friend, kissing a woman, kicking an enemy in the back, or simply screaming at strangers in the street?

People want to be published. They want their stories to be made into books that can be read by the rest of the 249,999,999 semi-literate American adults who are also writing novels. They want their hopes and dreams to be transmuted into novel form, to be admired by the rest of the us. They want to become famous. They want to become rich. They want to be interviewed by talk show hosts on national television. They want to see their books made into movies so they can watch their own names slide by during the opening credits. They want to become immortal, living forever in their work.

I wish them all good luck.

I also decline to participate.

If I decided to become a carpenter, which seems unlikely since my last carpentry project (a woodcut of my name that I made in a junior high shop class) somehow ended up catching fire while I was jig sawing it into existence, my competition would be limited. I would have to deal with the several hundred carpenters who live and work in San Francisco. I would paint my name, trade, and phone number on the side of my truck and people would call me. I would do my job. Those other few hundred carpenters might be better than me, but there would only be a few hundred of them. I could deal with that. I could find a place. I wouldn't have to compete against carpenters from Los Angeles or even Sacramento.

But if I took up my pen and decided to write a book, I would instantly find myself competing with 249,999,999 other writers. Much more than that, globally. Because I wouldn't just be competing with my fellow Americans; I would be competing with the world. Books have a habit of crossing borders, of being translated, of passing from hand to hand, of getting lost in an airport and picked up by someone new. They travel. I would be competing against every other writer on Earth.

There are many skilled writers around, and some of them pump out good books with intimidating regularity. And every time someone browsed a bookstore they would have to make a decision: do I read this book by this new guy I've never heard of, or do I read a novel by this famous novelist who has won 147 literary prizes and spends time on the bestseller list like it's her home and she's agoraphobic?

And that is not all. As a carpenter, I wouldn't have to compete against the guy who built Saint Peter's Basilica or the guy who built the pyramids. But as a writer I would have to compete not only with John Grisham and Stephen King, I would also have to compete against Arthur Conan Doyle and William Makepeace Thackeray. Because the great authors die, but their books live forever. When someone is browsing through the aisles at the bookstore they would have to walk past copies of *Catch-22*, *Pride and Prejudice*, *The Big Sleep, Moby Dick*, and *Richard III* to get to my book. Why would anyone do that?

On top of all this, there's the fact that writing correctly on a technical level is impossible. Did you know that we have six surviving signatures by Shakespeare and that he spelled his name differently in every single one of them? And did you further know that not once in his six signatures did he use the spelling that is currently accepted for his name? There was a time when there was no such thing as incorrect spelling. All you had to do was take a phonetic stab at your word and people would accept it. There was a time when grammar was a post-apocalyptic wasteland where there was no law. Those days are over. As the years have passed, we have become more democratic in everything but our language. Writing has become a minefield and you're almost certainly doing everything wrong, and so am I. In fact, you've probably already found all sorts of mistakes in this manuscript. I don't know what a dangling participle is, but I'm sure there are a bunch of them in in these pages. The same goes for split infinitives. I have only the vaguest of notions about how punctuation should be employed. When do I use a semicolon? This is one of the great mysteries of the age.

It would probably be best if you pretend that all the errors are a stylistic choice. Imagine that I am making mistakes on purpose because these mistakes give my protagonist character. They make him fallible and real. All the mistakes are evidence of my creative genius, not my inattention in high school English.

Writing a novel is an unforgivable act of arrogance, and it hurts me to realize that I'm going to have to write one.

Chapter 3

There is a lot to like about books. The actual contents of a book are the most important, obviously, but they are not all.

For one thing, books are walls. If you're out in public and, say, sitting on a bench at the park, when you pull that book out, crack it open, and begin to read, you are holding it like a shield. It's an object designed to protect you from the world. People see the book and they know you don't want to be talked to. You have walled yourself in from their attention. Your book is a small physical barrier that makes a powerful statement: leave me alone. I am a person who likes his solitude, and having a book lets me put up a wall wherever I am. As soon as I take my seat on a plane I pull out the biggest, most intimidating book in my bag and I open it, letting my seatmates know I would rather they keep their mouths shut. (It must be said in the favor of my seatmates, that most of the time they don't seem inclined to talk anyway.)

Also, if you have quite a lot of books filling up a large number of bookshelves along the walls of your home, that's a whole additional layer of insulation. Nothing keeps the cold out like a collection of the complete works of Anthony Trollope or James Patterson.

Books often smell wonderful. I own an old copy of *Heathen Days*, by H.L. Mencken. Not only is it a thoroughly entertaining memoir that I enjoyed reading very much, but it is also perhaps the best smelling object in my apartment. It is 70 years old and has decayed to a delicious ripeness. I don't know what kind of tobacco the book's previous owner smoked, but somehow *Heathen Days* soaked up the aroma of his pipe and when this scent mixed with the odor of old paper it created a perfume that almost makes me dizzy. Even stupid books can have a lovely scent. I own a copy of *The Alchemist* that smells fantastic.

Books can also be handy for home repairs. A few years ago, after a rough day, I collapsed into my mattress with a level of violence that my bed was unable to withstand. I lack the technical carpentry vocabulary to describe exactly what happened to my bed frame (essentially, one bit tore loose from another bit) but the important thing is that I was able to fix it up by stuffing a few stacks of books under the damaged part. (I used books that I didn't want people to see on my shelves. I have the whole Twilight series under there. Don't judge me. *Ulysses*, in contrast, stayed right out on the shelf where everyone can see it.)

Best of all, books are windows to the soul. Any one book by itself doesn't tell you much about a reader, but if you have the opportunity to look at a whole bookcase, you can learn a lot about the owner of that bookcase. Show me your bookcases and I'll know right away if we can be friends.

Let me stop there. I'm becoming a book bore. At this particular point in my story all you need to know about books is that they can act as force fields. As I mentioned in the second paragraph of this chapter, they keep people away. Unfortunately, a book is an imperfect defense, not as powerful as headphones, and a book will not protect you from the Garrulous Idiot, that person who does not read or even understand why a person would want to read, and therefore does not recognize a book for the big red stop sign that it is.

I ran into a Garrulous Idiot at Jiffy Lube recently. The Jiffy Lube waiting room is not an ideal environment for reading because there is a television in there and it is always turned to a show in which none of the waiting people have

17

the slightest interest. The volume is always turned all the way up, and the volume knob (the TV is invariably so old that it is the knobby kind) is broken off. Even worse, the Jiffy Lube waiting room attracts Garrulous Idiots like dead donkeys attract flies.

There were six other people in there with me on this occasion. Not a single one of us was looking at the television, but we all lacked the gumption to get up from our uncomfortable chairs and try to find a way to turn it off, or at least to turn it down. The other six were staring at their phones. I left my phone in my pocket and pulled out the paperback Michael Connelly novel I had started reading the night before. Detective Bosch was in big trouble with IA and I knew I would be turning the pages fast and steady until the final sentence. The roar of the television disappeared as my mind was pulled into the crime infested streets of Los Angeles.

But then the Garrulous Idiot walked in. Before he even said a word, I sensed him in the same way that Harry Potter can sense when a dementor is present. There was some life sucking force emanating from his aura that warned me that a disrespecter of book walls had entered and could make an assault at any moment. My brain left Detective Bosch as he chased down a suspect and I attempted to study this newcomer without looking at him beyond glancing at his feet. His shoes had Velcro instead of laces. This was a bad sign. I knew that to look at him was to invite him to sit next to me, so I pretended to read my book. I pretended so very hard.

He sat next to me anyway.

"I don't care what they say. I'm not going to ever use that synthetic oil. God made regular oil, so that's the only kind for me."

18

I focused on my book and pretended that I was reading so intently that I hadn't heard him. I knew that pretending wouldn't work; it hadn't worked with the girl at the bar in Chapter 1 after all, but a man has to use every defense at his disposal even when he knows things are hopeless. This is why we admire those who died at Thermopylae and The Alamo.

"It's just more money for nothin'. Do you use synthetic oil?"

I looked up now and acted like I hadn't realized he was talking to me. I didn't want him to think, or rather to know, that I had been deliberately ignoring him. Not that he would have cared very much. The Garrulous Idiot wants to talk, being listened to is of secondary importance.

"Oh, uh, I don't use synthetic oil either," I said before turning with a rude decisiveness back to my book.

"I always get the expensive gas though. You gotta get the expensive gas or your car won't perform. My brother, he always gets the cheap gas and his car just doesn't have any pep. That might be because it's Japanese. Honda. Also, his wife cheated on him, but that wasn't because of the car. She's bad but not so bad that she'd cheat because his car didn't have pep."

I sighed and closed my book, defeated, and we had a long conversation about the marital problems of the Garrulous Idiot's brother. Someone there is that doesn't respect a wall.

This is what I was thinking about as I sat at my table at Hunan Burrito, a Chinese/Mexican restaurant on the edge of Chinatown where they fill tortillas with things like fried rice and beef with broccoli. That probably doesn't sound very tasty, and you're right, it's not great, but sometimes the mediocrity of a restaurant can be a selling point. San

Francisco is a city for foodies, and there are a dozen good restaurants within walking distance of my office, but I preferred Hunan Burrito to all of them because unlike these other, better, restaurants, Hunan Burrito was always half empty. I know that if I eat at Hunan Burrito I will not have to wait for a table, and, even better, I will see no coworkers and will be able to read in peace. It is the place where I eat lunch whenever I have a good book going.

I was sitting at my usual table, reading *The Nix*, by Nathan Hill. I had purchased this book in hardback and regretted it as soon as the package arrived in the mail. It was heavy. Far too heavy. Lifting weights and reading books are activities that should be kept separate in my opinion, but that monster, Alfred A. Knopf, had managed to combine the two activities in this surprisingly heavy collection of 620 pages. Six hundred and twenty pages should not weigh this much, I thought as I pulled it out of the packaging. But I was enjoying the novel and had gone through the trouble of lugging it all the way from home to work, and then from work to the restaurant. At Hunan Burrito I was happy to set the book down on the table as I gnawed on my orange chicken burrito. Several drops of orange sauce had managed to splatter themselves across the pages and I knew that if anyone ever read this particular copy of *The Nix* in the future they would find the pages 317-326 welded together with a mysterious orange crust.

I actually wasn't reading anymore. I was trying to look like I was reading, but I wasn't. A couple minutes earlier a girl had walked in. Can I call her a girl? I mean, she was probably in her late twenties. That's too old to be a girl, really. Calling a grown woman a girl is no longer quite politically correct, but "woman" doesn't seem right either. She was just too cute. Very, very cute.

From the moment I first saw her I knew I had to talk to her. I didn't usually talk to strange women in Chinese/Mexican restaurants. In fact, never. I had never picked up a woman in a restaurant. Or anywhere else, now that I think of it. As I mentioned earlier, I'm not very outgoing. In the past I had only dated women who I met at work or who were introduced to me by friends, but one look at her and there was a click. Not only was she pretty, with her long black hair, large red mouth, and dark eyes, but something about her signaled to me that here was a kindred spirit. "Oh sure," you're probably saying, "every pretty girl is a kindred spirit." But I'm telling you this was different.

This feeling was given support as soon as she finished looking at the menu and pulled out a book of her own. She was reading *The Code of the Woosters*, by P.G. Wodehouse.

A book is a wall, yes, but sometimes a book is an invitation. A book can be a bridge between two people. If we have loved the same book there is a link between us. If you love *The Code of the Woosters* then we are well on our way to becoming friends.

I tried not to be obvious about it, but I watched her as she read. And as I watched I saw Wodehouse's words on her face. I saw them in her brightening eyes. I saw them in the soft lip bending smiles and toothy grins that flashed across her mouth. And when she actually laughed out loud I knew with absolute certainty that I couldn't let this girl leave without talking to her.

I hated to interrupt her, she was clearly enjoying herself, but I think Wodehouse would have approved, so I cleared my throat and said, "You seem to be enjoying that novel."

She was shaken out of her world of fiction. The smile vanished and suddenly I felt a leaden weight in my stomach. I had made a mistake. I had become the Garrulous Idiot. How could I think, for even a second, that she might prefer talking to me to reading P.G. Wodehouse? What awful arrogance! My behavior was Modern Dutch at its absolute worst. But then her eyes focused on me and her smile recovered a little and she said, "I love it. This is my third time reading it. It's so funny."

"I love it too. All the Jeeves books are great, but *The Code of the Woosters* is my favorite. I love the characters: Sir Roderick Spode, Gussy Fink-Nottle, Stinker Pinker, Madeline Bassett, the whole crew, really. It's pretty much perfect."

She visibly brightened. No celebrity's name has ever been dropped to greater effect than my dropping of the name "Gussy Fink-Nottle". She smiled and said, "Yes, it's not Modern Dutch at all." And then we both laughed at the inside joke she had made from the book that linked us.

Falling in love at first sight isn't cool anymore. It's an old-fashioned sort of thing to do. Like becoming a pirate or getting married. And I know that it's going to make me look bad to admit this, but fall in love at first sight is precisely what I had just done. In my defense, this woman was extraordinarily good looking. And that isn't all. She was also funny. I mean, did you hear here thing about Modern Dutch? I'll admit that it's something of an inside joke, only applicable to people who have read *The Code of the Woosters*, but that leads me to another point: she loved *The Code of the Woosters*. If a woman can share an inside joke based on one of your favorite books before you even know her name, that has to mean something, doesn't it?

And let me chuck in a few other details to illustrate what it is that I liked about her. Have I mentioned yet that she was wearing glasses? I love a girl in glasses. Not just any glasses, they have to have stylish frames, and the prescription can't be so powerful that they shrink her eyes

22

into tiny little beads that seem to be peering out from the porthole of a sinking submarine. Hers fit my preference perfectly. Cool black frames and lenses of a reasonable thickness. Her dark eyes could sparkle in their full glory.

Also, she was… well, now that I'm on the precipice of revealing this next detail, I hesitate. I mean, this isn't supposed to matter, after all. And, if I reveal this other thing about her that I found to make her more attractive… well, you may think me, uh, I don't know... creepy? Not creepy, maybe… Look, I'll just spit it out: SHE WAS ASIAN. I know race isn't supposed to enter into these things, but I like Asian women. I can't help it.

So, imagine a beautiful Asian woman in her late twenties to early thirties who reads P.G. Wodehouse, wears glasses, and has an amazing sense of humor. Clearly, I had no choice but to fall in love with her.

It's weird to fall in love with someone at first sight. I had never fallen in love before, at first sight or any other way. My previous relationships had always begun with the thought, "She's pretty and seems nice, I should date her and maybe we will fall in love." I never did fall in love with any of them (not, mind you, that there were a lot of them), and I don't think any of them fell in love with me either. Frankly, I had grown cynical about the whole idea of love. But now I could see where I had made my mistake. I had assumed that falling in love was something that I could somehow talk myself into overtime. Now I knew better. Now I knew that it had to be all at once or not at all. Love has to be unexpected, like a bolt of lightning in a snowstorm. Shakespeare was really onto something when he wrote, "Whoever loved that loved not at first sight?"

"I'm sorry I interrupted your reading," I said, and then immediately regretted it. I regretted it because I had once seen a television program with a self-described "pick up artist" who had written a book on how to pick up women, and his number one rule was to "ALWAYS ACT LIKE YOU ARE THE ONE DOING HER THE FAVOR BY ASKING HER OUT. NEVER SOUND UNCERTAIN OR APOLOGETIC." This guy was, needless to say, a creep (perhaps even creepy enough to be particularly attracted to Asian women), and I didn't want to give too much weight to his opinion, but I had to admit that there was a certain amount of sense in his rule.

"Oh, that's ok," she smiled, "I'm always glad to be interrupted by anyone who loves Wodehouse like I do."

"It is simply not possible to be unhappy when reading one of the Jeeves novels."

"I absolutely agree. Have you read any of his other books?"

"Loads. He wrote something like a hundred of them."

"I know. And it has always seemed strange to me that someone who wrote so much about lazy 'gentlemen of leisure' could be so hard working himself."

We discussed P.G. Wodehouse for several minutes. I won't put it all down here because unless you love Plum yourself, you probably wouldn't appreciate it. But I want to point out a few things that I noticed over the course of our conversation:

1. This woman had a charming voice. I like it when a woman has a voice that is feminine but has a bit of bite and growl to it. That's exactly what she had.

2. This woman was smart. Not only had she read a lot, but it quickly became clear that she knew how to use her mind; she didn't just stuff it with books.

3. Conversation with this woman was easy and fun.

4. This woman was beautiful. I know I have mentioned this already, but sometimes someone will strike you as good

looking when you first see them, but then, upon further observation, you notice all sorts of things wrong with them. For example, maybe from a different angle you can see that they don't have a chin, their face just seems to merge smoothly with their neck without any contour lines to suggest any kind of transition between neck and face. Or maybe when they laugh you discover that their teeth are just tiny little nubbins at the end of an unappealing broad expanse of gum. But this was not the case with her. She was lovely from every angle, and with any facial expression.

5. This woman loved books.

6. Forget this whole list. It presupposes that falling in love is somehow logical, that it is something that can be explained with a list. But I think love may be both illogical and undefinable. Besides, now that I have them down on paper, my reasons for falling for her look very thin.

Eventually we exhausted the subject of Wodehouse and I sensed that the time was right to present her with my name. "My name is Daniel, by the way."

"I'm Abigail. Or Abby. I answer to either."

Being named "Abigail" was another mark in her favor. It's a pretty name. And classic. I've always thought there was something in Walter Shandy's theories about the importance of names, and names that are not ridiculous are the optimal type. "Neither of us has parents who were interested in coming up with an original name, do we?"

"No, thank goodness. I knew a girl in high school named 'Pirate'. Can you imagine having to spend your whole life telling people that your name is 'Pirate'? It would be terrible."

"I knew a kid named 'Didgeridoo'."

"Poor guy."

"I know. It's terrible what parents do to their children. What do you do, by the way?"

"To my children?"

I laughed, which might have been more than her little joke deserved when you look at it objectively, but you can't see the delivery on the page. You've missed the excellent blank faced deadpan. Also, a woman's jokes always get a laugh boost when you have a crush on her. "No. Not to your children."

"I have no children, but I do have a job if that's what you were asking about."

"What is it?"

"Graphic design. I design things graphically. In a graphical way."

"That sounds interesting."

"No, it doesn't. Although, I really enjoy doing it. What do you do?"

"I…" and here I told her what I do. At too much length. I know my job is boring. It's so boring that I'm not even going to tell YOU what I do. It involves computers and shuffling papers around and such. Even mentioning that much is boring. If I'm going to write fiction, I need to learn to cut out the boring bits. That's what Elmore Leonard said, and he should know, I suppose. So I intend to cut out my job as much as I possibly can. Unfortunately, I did not cut out the details in my conversation with Abby. I spewed them over her like unwelcome sneezes of information. I realized I was boring her and beginning to destroy much of the good groundwork I had laid down with the early part of our conversation.

And then I panicked.

The problem was that I did not know Abby, and I did not know if I would ever see her again. I had no address, no phone number. I didn't even know her last name and if I lost her now I would probably lose her forever. This realization slowly crept into my brain as I described the sorts of spreadsheets I handled. I was talking too much and everything I said was suddenly unfathomably dull. I was supposed to be listening. That's what the pick-up artist guy on television had said, "Listen to whatever stupid stuff they say," he'd explained, "they'll be totally grateful and do anything you want later." I hate that I was thinking of that turd, but he was right again. And yet the words continued to come out of my mouth. I couldn't find a way to stop them. I had to do something! I had to shut up and get her talking! I had to ask her a question, any question, to shut my mouth and open hers.

So, I asked her the horrible question that is always on my own mind, "What's your novel about?" And immediately I knew that I had made a mistake. Yes, I had bought some time, and she would doubtless love to talk about her novel, which I was certain would be a good one. But when she got done detailing her delightful exchanges of dialogue and her shocking plot twists she would do the polite thing and ask me about my novel. I had set a trap for myself, and I knew it.

What I didn't know was exactly how quickly the trap would be sprung. And I was thunderstruck when instead of answering my question, she asked one of her own, "I'd rather hear you talk about yours. What's your novel about?"

Earlier in this book, I think it was Chapter 2, I bragged about my emotional even keel. "Even keel" is a cliché, and writers shouldn't use clichés. That's probably one of the first things that they teach you in those adult education writing classes that I will never take because I do not want to become a novelist. The reason they don't want you to use clichés is that clichés are boring and ugly. They smack of laziness and a lack of creativity. But I wonder if they don't do something worse than that: tempt the gods to anger. Because now, just a chapter after having bragged about my emotional even keel, the hand of Neptune had reached up from the bottom of the ocean and grabbed my ship by its supposedly steady keel. At first this was fun, and the exhilaration of love moved my ship through the water like a dolphin surfing on a wave. There was a slight chop on the sea, and I was getting tossed around a bit, but that just made things more fun. Is this what normal people felt like? I wondered. All these invigorating emotions? Delightful! But now Neptune, who had grown tired of playing with my ship, threw a storm that immediately flooded my vessel and threatened to bring me down into the depths.

"What's my novel about?" I repeated in a dazed voice, as if I wasn't certain I had heard her correctly.

"Yeah. What's it about?"

As you know, unless you skipped the first twenty pages or so of this book and just started right here, I didn't have a novel, or any ideas for a novel. I couldn't admit my shameful secret to her though, so I looked around the restaurant, remembering how many writing prompts Kaiser Soze had found in that room at the police station. Was my book about a Chinese-Mexican restaurant? No, too on the nose. Plates? Forks? No and No. Falling in love unexpectedly with a beautiful Asian girl? No! Then my eye darted out the window of the restaurant and I saw a homeless man pushing a shopping cart.

"THE HOMELESS!" I shouted like a game show contestant who has suddenly come up with an answer where a moment before there was only a blankness haunted by the sound of a ticking clock.

"Oh? What about the homeless?"

"How bad it is to be homeless."

"Have you done research on the subject?"

"Yes." This was not an absolute lie. I had just that morning read an article in the Chronicle about how the city had hired additional workers to help clean up excrement left in the street by the homeless. I thought I could count that as research, but at the same time, it felt weak, so I also blurted out, "PLUS I'M GOING TO LIVE ON THE STREET FOR A MONTH." What? What did I just say?

"Like George Orwell spending time as a tramp?"

Ahhhh, and we were back to books. I was more comfortable with books, so I shook off some of my panicked despair and said, "Yes! I love him! *Down and Out in Paris and London* is so good. He's my inspiration."

And then we talked about George Orwell for a while. It was nice to talk about Orwell. Very relaxing to consider the growth of technologies and politics that make Big Brother a real possibility after the miseries of those panicked moments where I had to come up with a novel. Had I really said I was writing a book? About the homeless? And that I was going to live on the street? Insanity! But these dark thoughts dissipated quickly, as if they were storm clouds dissolved by the warmth of Abby's sunshine. (Gross. Being in love makes a man write terrible things.) We were soon laughing again, chatting of this and that. I was about to ask her for her cell number when suddenly we discovered a man looming over our table.

"Why are we eating at this disgusting place?" he asked Abby.

His question had sounded rude to me, but she answered him with equanimity, "It's quiet. I knew you would be late and I wanted a chance to read in peace. I walk by this restaurant sometimes and it looked like a place where I could read without interruption."

"Oh?" he asked as he cast a hostile glance in my direction.

"This Daniel. He noticed I was reading the *Code of the Woosters* and we have been talking about how it's one of our favorite books."

"I haven't read it," the man said as he sat down, "I only like serious literature."

I wondered if this man, this incarnation of Sir Roderick Spode, could possibly be Abby's boyfriend. He spoke to her with a firm tone of possession, but it seemed impossible to me that such a gorgeous, intelligent, confident, and amusing woman could allow herself to become attached to an atrocious Spode. He was handsome, I'll give him that, with his thick brown hair cut into a hipster sort of wave, his neatly trimmed beard, his smooth tan skin and a body that rippled with sculptured muscle under his tight V-neck tee shirt. Nothing is worse than a beautiful man who is liked by the girl you're in love with.

As the beautiful Spode sat down with us, he placed a book on the table. The cover said, "*Promethean Nipples: A Collection of Stories by Chadwick Blowington.*"

I decided to be polite, so I ignored the slight against Wodehouse, pumped an ingratiating smile onto my lips, pointed at the book and said, "Well, that looks like some serious literature. Is it any good?"

"I like to think so," he answered in a tone that let me know he didn't care about my opinion of his book, "I wrote it."

"Chad publi…" Abby began before being cut off.

"Chadwick! Please, Abigail, I go by Chadwick now!"

"Chadwick published his first collection of short stories a month ago."

I'd known him for less than two minutes, and yet, I had never disliked anyone quite as much as I disliked Chadwick. Two things were clear at this moment: This guy was Abby's boyfriend and he wanted me to leave the two of them alone.

30

I only had one card to play to keep myself at the table, and in Abigail's presence, a little longer. So I played it, "Now that you've published those stories, what are you working on? A novel?"

Of course he was working on a novel. A collection of short stories is a sadly second-rate sort of thing compared to a novel. No storywriter worth his printer cartridges doesn't want to write a novel. It's like how every actor would really like to direct, and every burger flipper would really like to work the counter. For a moment I could see Chadwick struggle. Did he want me to leave or did he want to tell me about his book? Did he hate me more than he loved his book? When he asked himself the question in that way the answer was perfectly obvious, and he launched into his story.

His novel began with the primordial ooze. "A warm and sludgy puddle teeming with amino acids that were as yet formless, and unorganized. Then, a bolt of lightning set the stony cauldron boiling." Some novels begin *in medias res*, and some begin in the Cambrian period. I groaned as I realized that Chadwick's story was the second kind. But I had brought this upon myself so I decided I might as well get comfortable. And it would be worth it if somehow I could stay with Abby a little longer, and maybe find out a thing or two about her. Her phone number, in particular.

As you have probably guessed, a simple creature sprang to life in Chadwick's puddle. It was fruitful and multiplied. Soon there were trilobites wiggling their way through the mud. And then dinosaurs, but they were annihilated by an asteroid. I thought that the story would take a leap forward at this juncture, but it did not. Instead, Chadwick traced the long history of that asteroid, from its early formation out of the dust that would become the solar system, to its collision with another asteroid in the Kuiper Belt that would change its orbit, and then a series of collisions during the Late Heavy Bombardment that altered its orbit even further and set it on the path that would eventually lead to its impact with Earth. But not until another four billion years any many pages of poetic prose had passed.

Chadwick went on and on. And on. And then on some more. Eventually, a hero arose out of this history, as if all creation, from that first creeping lifeform, though the wooly mammoths, to the present day, had struggled into existence, had reproduced, and had died, for no reason other than the birth of the novel's hero. And that hero was Chadwick Blowington. He didn't even bother to give his novelistic alter ego a fictional name. He just went ahead and called him "Chadwick Blowington." He was a man who could not get enough of himself.

The asteroid that annihilated those dinosaurs sixty-five million years ago set in motion a chain of events that led to the birth of the great misunderstood genius who was Chadwick Blowington. God had plucked that rock out of its orbit beyond Pluto and flung it at the Earth for no reason but to make the world safe for Chadwick Blowington, to allow him to show his superiority to all the other pathetic hairless apes who couldn't understand him because they were as blockheaded as the defunct race of Neanderthals. He was the next step in evolution, the final step, the step that would bring perfection.

I mean, maybe it wasn't in quite those words, but that was the gist I got out of it, and it was nauseating.

I had been routed, and I knew it. I had felt a connection between myself and Abby, and I didn't think I was deluding myself when I imagined that she felt it too. I had fallen in love with her, to put it with embarrassing honesty. But what could I do? She was already taken, and by a published

author no less. Sure, they were just short stories, and
nobody would ever read them.   But still, what could I do? I
withdrew from the table, a defeated man.

Chapter 4

After all that had happened, I couldn't go straight back to work. You can't find the love of your life and lose her again in the space of an hour and then just go back to work like your pathetic existence hadn't just been torn down to the foundations. I roamed the streets, pressing into Chinatown, slowly shuffling, impervious to all the weird, fishy smells of that neighborhood. I muttered nonsense under my breath. At one point tears bubbled up from my subterranean depths and clouded my vision, but without ever quite forming drops and running down my face. It was clear that the days of my even keel were over.

I was in a sort of shock and I tried to step out of myself, to leave my body along with my emotions for a second and just think rationally. I stopped walking and the crowds of Chinese people and tourists flowed around me as if I was a boulder and they were a mountain stream. I clawed my way out of my own mind and hovered in the air above my inert body.

Just look at that guy, I thought, as I peered down at myself. Look at that sad face, those watery eyes, those sunken cheeks, and that slightly quivering chin. What a pathetic spectacle. Ridiculous. Where is that rational man whose company I have always enjoyed? That placid, content person? What has changed in the past hour? When you really look into it, nothing. Nothing has changed. Have I become poorer? No. Have my children died? No. Have I suddenly had children? No. Have I been diagnosed with a terminal illness? No. What happened? I met a girl, that's it. Why was I standing there moping like some drama queen on a crowded sidewalk in Chinatown when all that had happened in the past hour is that I'd met a girl. Yes, she was pretty, Asian, wore glasses, and loved P.G. Wodehouse, but still, this was ridiculous.

I hesitated before allowing my mind to climb back into the brain of that pathetic man quivering on the sidewalk, but there was nowhere else for it to go, so in the end my mind went back into the only space where it would fit. But as my mind clicked back into place, I suddenly had a plan. If I truly loved this woman, then, well, I wasn't going to give her up, boyfriend or not. I would find a way get her to break up with that odious Spode she called her boyfriend, I would win her over, and then I would do the old fashioned thing and marry her. I would do all this even if it meant writing a novel. And I knew that writing a novel would be key to the whole enterprise. I would one up Chadwick Blowington at his own game; I would become a published novelist. I would win Abby's love and respect.

As these bold thoughts entered my brain, I felt a wave of confidence wash over me. In reading the paragraph above you may have noticed that my plan was lacking in detail. I was like a general who simply yelled "ATTACK" upon sight of the enemy without bothering about any of the details that might make the attack a success. How was I going to line up the troops, what should the cavalry do, where was I going to position the artillery? I didn't know. But I did know one thing, that to successfully win Abby over, I would have to be able to find her when I was ready to make the move. I needed a phone number or an address, or the name of the place where she worked. I was furious with myself for leaving the restaurant without getting some kind of helpful detail. I hurried back now to find her.

The restaurant was empty when I got there. No Abby. Not even a Chadwick. Just a couple flies licking some brown goo that had spilled out of somebody's Mongolian beef burrito and onto the floor. Depressing. Oh well. I would find her, but that was a problem to be solved later.

Chapter 5

I wouldn't say I skipped back to the office, but I wasn't trudging either. I was taking long, serious, purposeful, manly strides. I had plans percolating in my head, and it was time to start putting them into action. The first thing I had to do was to get some time off, so I marched right into Glen Strop's office and demanded it. "Demanded" is probably too strong a word. Glen is a friendly sort of boss, and he's very much inclined to give his employees what they ask for if it's possible. I knocked at the wall outside his office as I walked in.

"Do you have a minute?" I asked.

"Sure," he said as he put down a sheet of paper he had been reading. Glen was a slick looking man who always wore tailored suits (sans tie), gold cufflinks, and an enormous gold watch. His thick brown hair was swept dramatically back in a way that made it appear that he was moving forward at some tremendous speed and his sharp nose was helping to slice the air in front of him as he went.

His office was decorated in the Spartan style. There were no knickknacks, no objects visitors could fondle as they talked to him, no awards made of glass and metal to commemorate services he had done for the corporation (although he had done many, and had received several such awards) and no family pictures of any kind. His desk never held anything but his computer, any paper document he might be actively using at the moment, and a fabulously expensive pen made out of gold and mahogany that was as thick as a Costco hot dog. His office gave you the impression that he was prepared to abandon the building and take a better offer from a competing company at any moment without having to pack a lot of bric-a-brac with him when he went. He could just grab that pen and go.

Aside from the pen, the only object in the entire room that could be classified as a decoration was a book. Books, in addition to all their other qualities, can make great decorations. There is nothing in the world as pleasant to look at as a favorite book that also has a beautiful cover.

Glen's book, however, was by no means a pleasant one to look at. The cover, which was done up in a sort of dramatically expressionist style, depicted a man and a woman, both dressed sharply in dark business attire, striding forward towards some gloriously lucrative future. Each one was clutching a bag of money while hundred-dollar bills rained down on them from, one can only assume, the gods themselves. They looked like caricatures of capitalists from a Soviet propaganda poster. Between these two figures there was a third person, a man, dressed in a suit of armor and brandishing a bloody sword with a decapitated head impaled on the tip.

The book was called "*Genghis Khan: The Business Secrets of the Leader Who Forged the First Global Network*." It was a business book, but written in the form of the novel, and it told the story of Genghis Khan travelling through time to help one of his descendants, now living in Silicon Valley, to launch a tech start-up called "Twerpy". I read the first ten pages of it once. I don't think very many people got past those first ten pages, and for a while there were stacks of Glen's book piled up in the remainder bins of bookstores across America. I have to assume they have all been pulped by now and that their atoms have been rearranged into better selling books. But Glen was proud of his work; he'd had one copy framed, and that framed copy was hung in the center of the otherwise blank wall behind him.

You'd think that a man who wrote a book called *Genghis Khan: The Business Secrets of the Leader Who*

Forged the First Global Network would be a brutal and bossy sort of boss, but Glen was not. One of the chapters in his book was called, "Taking Care of Your Soldiers." I haven't actually read that chapter since it sits in a portion of the book beyond the ten pages that I was able to get through, but I have to assume it says that you should be nice to those soldiers, because Glen was always nice to us.

I closed the door as I walked in and Glen said, "Uh oh, a closed-door meeting. I must be in trouble."

I smiled, and even gave him a chuckle, before assuring him, "No, but it's sort of personal." I sat across from him and he pushed his computer monitor out of the way to look at me.

"Personal? Are you alright?"

"I'm fine, but, you remember how I'm not working on a novel?"

"Yes," he answered grimly.

"Well, I have an idea now."

"You do!" He was legitimately happy for me, just as Genghis Khan would have been if one of his warriors had told him he was working on a novel. "That's great news!" Glen was well aware of my writing problem, and for as long as I had known him he had urged me to get a book started.

"Yeah, except, uh, I'm going to need some time off to get it going."

"To write?"

"No. To research."

"How much time off?"

"Three weeks?" I said this in a questioning and apologetic tone, and he let out a low and toothy whistle in response.

"Three weeks! What kind of research is this? What's your book about? You know, I didn't take any time off when I wrote *Genghis Khan: The Business Secrets of the*

Leader Who Forged the First Global Network. I did that on my own time." Glen worked his book into every conversation, but on this occasion he had a more substantial pretext than usual.

"I know, but, I, uh, you know how hard it has been for me to be creative. My tank of inspiration is dry, and I need experience to fill it up."

"What kind of experience?"

"Well, I want to write a novel about being homeless, so I'm going to live on the street for a while."

He looked at me with incredulity stamped into his face, "You're going to sleep in the streets? Panhandle? Get drunk and stoned in public?"

"Yeah, more or less."

"Let me ask you a question."

"Sure."

"Did J.R.R. Tolkien have to visit Mordor to write *The Lord of the Rings*?"

"No."

"Did Jonathan Swift have to visit Lilliput to write *Gulliver's Travels*?"

"Well, no, but…"

"Did I have to visit Mongolia to write *Genghis Khan: The Business Secrets of the Leader Who Forged the First Global Network*?"

"I don't thin…"

"Then why do you think you have to live on the street to write about what life is like for a homeless guy? Writing is an act of imagination! It comes from the mind! See that book up there, my framed copy of *Genghis Khan: The Business Secrets of the Leader Who Forged the First Global Network*?"

"Yes."

"Do you think I did any research whatsoever in writing that book?"

"I assumed that…"

"Wrong! Wrong! It is the child of my brain! Of my heart! Those are the organs you write with!"

"Sure, but readers seem to appreciate it when you get the details right."

This gave him pause, and I think that for a moment the image of thousands of copies of *Genghis Khan: The Business Secrets of the Leader Who Forged the First Global Network* being pulped flashed before his mind. "Still. Three weeks is a lot. I mean, our policy is to only allow vacations of up to two weeks except in cases of maternity or paternity leave. Have you recently had a child?"

"No. But I really need this. Even beyond the research, I need the inspiration. You know how boring my life has been. I have finally realized that what I need in order to write is experience. Maybe you never went to Mongolia, but you had years of business experience before writing *Genghis Khan.*"

"That's true. Hmmmm. There is also *pet*ernity leave. Have you recently acquired a pet?"

"No, but I could buy a hamster or a goldfish or something if I had to."

He grew quiet and looked at me deeply. "You know, 'A Good General Takes Care of His Soldiers.' That's chapter 14 of *Genghis Khan: The Business Secrets of the Leader Who Forged the First Global Network.*"

"I know."

"So, I'm going to work this out with you. If you will make a donation of $200 to an animal shelter of some kind, I will consider it pet ownership for our purposes and give you three weeks off, starting next Monday if you can get your affairs in order by then and take the time without disrupting things too much."

I assured him that Monday would be perfect and thanked him sincerely.

As I was about to leave, he said, "You know, 'Genghis Khan Never Took a Day Off.' That's the title of chapter 5 of *Genghis Khan: The Business Secrets of the Leader Who Forged the First Global Network*. Don't stay away too long. You don't want people to get used to not having you around."

Chapter 6

Being homeless is not safe. I read somewhere that about 3,500 people live on the streets of San Francisco, and 87 of them died last year. I realize that "I read somewhere" isn't a great source but I'm afraid to google the real numbers because they may be even worse. There's a lot that can happen to a person who is sleeping on the streets, without any walls to protect him from ne'er-do-wells who rove in bands through the streets of any city. He could be robbed, he could be beaten, he could be mocked, bullied, vilified, mistreated in multifarious ways. Accidents can befall him too, he can be run over by a garbage truck while he sleeps behind a dumpster, fall through a floor while squatting in an abandoned building. Disease is lurking out there as well, exposure to the elements, eating contaminated food. All these worms were wriggling through my mind as I packed my backpack in preparation for my great expedition, filling it with a sweater, a journal, some pens, a sleeping bag, and a bit of cash to get me started while I ginned up the courage to panhandle.

The article about homeless deaths was not very specific about how these people died. It didn't include the names or life stories of any of the bodies hauled out of the gutter by the sanitation department. It didn't even say what had killed them, though I'm certain the usual suspects could be implicated here: alcoholism, murder, heart failure, reopened war wounds, strokes, accidents, suicides and heartbreak. There are too many ways to die. San Francisco is a place that pays close attention to trends, however, so no doubt some of the homeless were carried away by stylish diseases like aids or breast cancer.

When I first arrived in the city, fresh off the plane from Normalcy, I used to study the homeless who littered the sidewalks of Market Street. They would construct crude shelters in the recessed doorways of closed businesses. They made walls with discarded refrigerator boxes and stolen shopping carts, and they furnish their shelters with strips of cardboard upholstered with dirty rags. They built ragged tent cities under I-80 onramps, or just collapsed on benches in Golden Gate Park. They would lay there all day long, lost in drug-induced stupors, sucking in their own fecal miasma with every breath, apparently straddling the line between life and death, and clearly beyond caring which way they went. Meanwhile, everybody just walked by, pretending not to see any of it.

Of course, every once in a while, one of the homeless wouldn't lie meekly out of the way. Instead he would be sprawled right across the middle of the sidewalk with slightly cracked eyelids showing two red quarter-moons of eyeball, his body twisted unnaturally at every joint. "Is he dead" I would wonder? Perhaps he was dead, but what could I do about it? Should I poke him with a stick? Should I hold a mirror up to his mouth (with all its blackened, cigarette-butt stumps for teeth) and check for breath? Someone else, I was sure, would handle the situation. I paid my taxes so that someone else would deal with this sort of thing. This attitude now seemed appallingly selfish.

Was I really about to join these people? Was this really the life I was committed to living for three weeks?

I know what I was doing was unwise. I was turning my back on my warm home and loaded pantry because I wanted to impress a girl. A girl who I might never even see again. Everybody knows that men do stupid things for women, but not me. My romantic gestures had always been limited to cards and flowers.

I stepped out the door on my first day as a street person looking ragged in the secondhand clothes I had bought for the occasion, but I was pretty clean. I didn't look or smell particularly like a bum, and I knew I would have to work some grime into my outfit before I could be convincing. I experienced a strange exhilaration as the door clicked shut behind me. I felt like Meriwether Lewis, like Columbus, like Neil Armstrong. I had begun my grand voyage and every sail was catching wind as waves of glory broke gracefully under my bow.

I live on Jackson in Pacific Heights and the easiest thing to do was to simply give into gravity and walk down the slope towards the Bay. I crossed Union Street, where the well-heeled were drinking coffee and talking about whatever it is the well-heeled talk about, and then I proceeded towards Lombard. When I arrived at Lombard I turned right and headed towards Fisherman's Wharf. There are always panhandlers down there, bumming spare change of the herds of tourists, and I planned to join them.

When I had left my home that morning, I was wearing every scrap of clothing I intended to take with me. The night before had been clear and cold, and the morning sun had not been out long enough to raise the temperature. By the time I had walked a few blocks along Lombard, however, I was wet with sweat.

Just the fact that I wasn't going to return to my own home, to sleep in my own bed, changed the feeling of the streets for me. Somehow the sights and smells became more vivid. I found myself looking into the faces of the people I passed and wondered which of them would be willing to give me a dollar if I asked for one. I didn't ask anybody yet, but it was already on my mind. I looked around for places to sleep. Could I sleep in some bushes? In an alley? Should I be looking for a box or a discarded painter's drop cloth that I could use for shelter? I already wished I had brought a tent.

Nothing had changed for me, not yet, not really, but somehow everything felt a little different. I was tingling with a strange energy and I began to actually believe that maybe I would get some inspiration from this project I had undertaken.

An old song popped into my brain and I began to hum it before realizing that limiting myself to a timid hum went against the spirit of what I was trying to accomplish, so I began to sing instead. Loud. And in the style of Frank Sinatra whose swinging version of the tune I preferred:

I got plenty of nothing
And nothing's plenty for me
I got no car - got no mule
I got no misery

Folks with plenty of nothing
They've got a lock on the door
Afraid somebody's going to rob 'em
While there out a-making more - what for?

No one bothered to turn their head, and I realized that I had always spent a lot of time worrying about the opinions of other people, while in fact most people are never going to care about me one way or another. Go ahead and do what you want. No one is looking and no one cares. Especially in San Francisco. Open your pipes and sing as loud as you can. This will not make you look particularly eccentric here.

I walked slowly, rested often, and arrived at the Wharf just before noon. I ambled past steaming pots of crabs. The warm sea smell of boiling shellfish crawled in through my nose and scratched the naked interior of my stomach. My gut began to growl. Tourists in Alcatraz tee shirts were standing around eating seafood sandwiches and drinking Coca-Cola. The heavy odor of clam chowder was thick in the air. The cereal I had eaten that morning had moved down the line by this time and left my stomach with nothing to keep it occupied. My belly snarled and I decided that I could put off panhandling while I ate a light lunch.

The steaming crabs were clearly outside the bounds of my strict budget, so I located the nearest McDonald's. I was able to get two cheeseburgers and a cup of water for under three dollars. The cup had been inadequately waxed and felt fragile and damp in my hand as I carried it to the nearest open table. I normally remove the pickle from my hamburger and tossed it aside, but this time I didn't. Every calorie counted now.

After lunch I went back outside to consider my immediate future. It was a weekday in the off season, but large crowds still roamed the sidewalks around the wharf. People were buying Golden Gate Bridge shot glasses and pornographic postcards to send back home to Wichita and Kankakee. Thuggish groups of teens moved like clumps of fat in the bloodstream, looking for the opportunity to cause a problem. Asians, whites, Latinos, blacks, people from every walk of life strolled along the sidewalks, gazing through the open storefronts at the impressive array of garbage offered up for sale inside.

I wandered around for a while before I realized that I was only wandering because I couldn't bring myself to beg. So far being on the street had consisted of nothing but a feeling of freedom. I didn't have to go to work. I didn't have to take any phone calls, read any emails, or look at any social media sites. I had left my phone at home. Homelessness was all upside. But this wasn't supposed to be a vacation. I was going to have to do some things that I didn't want to do, and right at the top of that list was panhandling. Asking strangers for money. Begging.

I didn't want to do it. The thought of begging made me sick. But if I was serious about researching this stupid book, I was going to have to do it. So, I looked around in the dumpster behind a seafood restaurant and pulled out a scrap of cardboard box. I had brought a black Sharpie with me and I used it to write, "I'm at the end of my rope. Please Help."

With my sign completed I walked to a busy corner and sat down, but I had the message of the sign facing my body and not the street. Somehow, I couldn't bring myself to turn it around so that the humiliating words would be seen by the passing tourists. Up until this point I could have been just another reveler supping at the tourist trap's fleshpots. I was perhaps dressed a little shabby, but I was clean, and there was nothing about my appearance that could clearly brand me with the stigma of poverty. In turning the sign towards the public and asking for a handout I would be taking the final leap and would plummet to the bottom rung of society. I would be a beggar.

I needed to turn the sign around. I couldn't bear to do it. I needed to turn the sign around. I couldn't bear to do it. I needed to turn the sign around. I couldn't bear to do it.

As I sat there warring with myself a pair of legs stopped in front of me with the toes pointed in my direction. The legs were clad in blue jeans and the feet at the bottom of them were shoed with a pair of expensive looking sneakers.

I did not look up.

A dollar bill which had been folded twice fluttered down like a green snowflake and landed on the cement in front of my crotch. The legs moved on. I sat there for a moment longer, staring at the folded face of George Washington as a wave of shame washed over me. I snatched up the bill and stuffed it into my pocket. That was it. That was all the begging I could handle for one day. I knew I would not be able to ask a stranger for money again until I truly was desperate. The ordeal had been more humiliating than I had imagined. Only hunger could drive me to ever do it again.

I backed away from the corner and threw my sign into a trashcan. The receptacle was overflowing with a variety cups and wrappers, the assorted detritus of the tourist industry, and it was only with a frenzied effort that I was able to cram my own addition into the cylinder. I was sweating again as I hurried away from the wharf.

Chapter 7

The day was nowhere near over and I found myself burdened with an overabundance of worthless time. I had no work. I had no television. I had no computer, no housecleaning, no health club membership, no phone, and no books. I didn't have a single one of the potential distractions that could be offered by my apartment or a hundred-dollar bill. I had nothing to do.

I drifted about like a waterlogged corpse on the Mississippi and after a couple of hours found myself lying on the lawn of Moscone Park. One of the softball fields was occupied with a couple teams of senior citizens competing against each other. Children played tag a hundred feet away from me. Dog owners walked their animals across the grass and stooped to pick up lumpy dog turds with clear plastic sandwich bags. Nobody noticed me. I was just another part of the landscape.

I stood up and searched the park's trash cans until I found a newspaper. Things were happening in the world. There were wars and rumors of wars. The Giants had made a good off-season acquisition. Somebody I had never heard of was speculating that somebody else I had never heard of was going to be nominated for a government post that I hadn't known existed. Every once in a while you will see a homeless person sitting on the curb with their eyes locked on a copy the *Chronicle*. I used to think it strange that they could sit there calmly reading about current events. Their own lives, I thought, should be current event enough. Why would a man care about the stabbing of a socialite or a coup in Africa when he was scrounging for food every day? When you're going to spend the night outdoors in the rain, does it really matter who has the best record in the Western Conference? Apparently, it does matter, at least to the extent

50

that poring over such intrinsically worthless information serves to alleviate the deadly boredom of transient existence.

Darkness came by degrees and the temperatures in the clear evening began to drop. The park was soon empty. I was alone and began to feel out of place. Police don't like to see the homeless lurking in parks after dark. It occurred to me, as the evening began to deepen, that I wasn't going to be able to spend the night on the street.

The thought of being out in the noisy darkness of a city night was suddenly terrifying to me. Before, in the comfort and safety of my own apartment, spending a night in the bracing San Francisco air had not seemed an unendurable hardship. I'd been camping before. For a brief period in my youth I had actually been a Boy Scout. What was the problem then? The problem was that sleeping outdoors in the city suddenly seemed much more dangerous than camping out in Eisenhower State Park with Troop 763. The thought of being beaten, murdered, or robbed of my few precious dollars was appalling to me. I would have to ease into the brutal reality of my project by degrees. I needed more daylight time on the streets to toughen me up for the night.

What to do then? Clearly, I could not afford to spend money on even the seediest of motels, and going home was out of the question. My whole project would be ruined only hours after starting if I gave up now. I would be guilty of a humiliating act of cowardice. My only option was to leave the city for the countryside. I would walk across the Golden Gate Bridge and sleep somewhere in the hills on the other side.

On my way out of town I bought a loaf of cheap wheat bread, a small jar of peanut butter, and a bottle of water. Peanut butter, it turns out, is pricey, and after this spree I didn't have much money left. The bottle of water may seem

51

like an unwarranted extravagance for a homeless person, but I needed the bottle itself to carry water. I was camping out, after all, and every good Boy Scout knows that the most important item in a Scout's backpack is his trusty canteen.

A couple hours later I found a thicket of bushes on the lee of a Marin Headlands hill and I made my camp there. The hill and its shrubbery provided some protection from the chilling Pacific breezes, but if it had rained, as it frequently did that time of year, I would have been soaked to the bone. Even without rain the night proved to be a rough one. Though I did have some shelter, wind penetrated my sleeping bag and pushed the warmth from my body. Even though I was wearing every stitch of clothing I had brought with me, I still shivered. The ground was hard, rock covered, and uneven. I tossed and turned all night, but the only effect of all the movement was to ensure that no part of my body escaped bruising.

I have never been a good sleeper. The slightest noise, the smallest irritation, or the most distant hint of an unpleasant dream instantly brings me up from the depths of sleep. When you look up at a dark building at three in the morning and see one light turned on up there on the fifth floor and you wonder, "Who is up at this hour?" it's probably me. I'm up there. Awake. I'm probably too tired to read so I'm staring bleary eyed at the Cartoon Network while shoving some Ben & Jerry's into my mouth in the hope that it will have some narcotic effect that will help me drift off at last. And it probably won't work.

People who don't suffer from insomnia will never get it. They'll never understand what it is like to stare up at the ceiling getting angry with the whole concept of sleep, becoming bitterly jealous of the person breathing deeply in the bed next to you, feeling tempted to go out and run twenty miles in the probably vain hope that it will wear you down to

52

the point that sleep becomes inevitable. How does the first glimmer of a rising sun strike you? Do you think it's a beautiful thing? A reminder of God's love or the inherent beauty of nature? A sunrise fills the average person with hope and awe; it fills an insomniac with bitterness and despair.

My first night as a homeless man was worse than any of those thousands of other terrible nights I have suffered through because of my insomnia. I did drift off a few times but was repeatedly jerked awake within minutes by the sharp jab of a rock, a freezing gust of wind, or the harsh stab of a nightmare. Each time I awoke I immediately became aware of the hum emanating from the peninsula. I would turn towards San Francisco and gaze at the halo of light the city threw against the low clouds hanging over it like alien spaceships with evil intent. It should have been a beautiful sight, but it was not. The city seemed filled with menace.

I thought about Abigail. I wondered if she was asleep. I wondered if she knew what insomnia was like. Wondered if she would turn out to be a blanket hogger.

Dawn found me stuffed as deeply into my sleeping bag as I could go. I was fully awake, lying in the fetal position with my knees to my chest. I was shivering slightly. When I was a Boy Scout, it was at this point I would have made a fire and boiled up some hot cocoa, but I didn't have any cocoa. Nor did I have matches.

Chapter 8

After walking back across the bridge this morning, I
meandered down the hill to Crissy Field and sat in the grass.
Crossing the bridge had been an exhausting experience. It is
a long walk, and I battled fierce Pacific winds the entire
distance. Worse than the distance and the wind, however,
was the extreme tension of a Golden Gate Bridge crossing.
Six lanes of cars and trucks zoomed by at fifty miles an hour.
It's like walking on the shoulder of a busy highway. In fact,
it *is* walking on the shoulder of a busy highway. Tourists,
keeping as far from the road as they could, pretended to have
a good time, but I could see the fear in their eyes every time
an enormous northbound Greyhound roared by, missing
them by only a few feet.

Crissy Field was a relaxing counterpoint to the mad rush
of the bridge. The only noises to be heard there were the
light thuds of jogger's feet across the paved waterfront path
and the laughter of children racing bicycles. There was less
wind and in the surprising warmth of the sunny February day
the breeze almost felt pleasant as it dried the sweat from my
face. I turned my gaze to the bay. The water was placid and
empty except for a scattering of triangular sails and one
slowly moving barge. My view of Sausalito was blurred by
an ethereal haze that emanated from the water.

I felt like an interloper. I no longer belonged in the
civilized world. Crissy Field is a place where few of the
homeless intrude. I still didn't feel quite like a bum, but I
was dirty and lugging all my possessions in a backpack, and
I clearly did not belong in the company of all the beautiful
people around me. My presence was making the young
mothers and nannies uncomfortable. They threw worried
glances at me from time to time, no doubt wondering how

their bum-free sanctuary had come to be profaned by the likes of me.

After dozing on the warm sand for about a half hour I moved on. I had no specific destination, so I roamed about the city with no goal other than the abatement of my boredom. By the midafternoon I found myself on Polk Street. The Nob Hill section of Polk Street is in a good neighborhood. There the street is lined with small stores, coffee shops, and pleasant cafes. As you go down the hill these businesses give way, by degrees, to restaurants that are only a quarter-step ahead of the health inspectors. Then these seedy establishments are replaced by dingy liquor stores and pornographic video centers. And finally, at the end of the street, you find the golden dome of City Hall and the heart of the Civic Center. San Francisco was clearly laid out by a cynic. City Hall is below King Kwan's Palace O' Porn on the Polk Street respectability spectrum.

The San Francisco Public Library, just across the Plaza from City Hall, is a rock where the shipwreck survivors known as the homeless wash up every day. It's warm there, it is much more comfortable to poop in the library's toilets than in the rain behind a dumpster or in the bushes at a park, and as long as you are quiet and don't fall asleep they won't kick you out.

You don't see the homeless in used bookstores nearly as often. Used bookstores attract weirdos of various descriptions, as George Orwell noticed when he worked in a second hand bookshop, "In a town like London there are always plenty of not quite certifiable lunatics walking the streets, and they tend to gravitate towards bookshops, because a bookshop is one of the few places where you can hang around for a long time without spending any money." The same goes for San Francisco. Lots of weirdos to lounge

55

around in bookshops, not spending any money. I am, I suppose, one of these weirdos.

Orwell, in that same essay, says that people imagine secondhand bookstores as "a kind of paradise where charming old gentlemen browse eternally among calf-bound folios." He then goes on to paint working in a bookshop as a kind of hell on earth, which is pretty much how he paints all jobs in his writing. Police work, cooking in a French restaurant, coal mining, fighting Spanish fascists, selling books, all of them are hell. For Orwell, a used bookstore is a place where you spend your entire day answering stupid questions and selling trash to the semi-literate while occasionally sweeping dead flies off the inventory.

The crime novelist Lawrence Block, on the other hand, has written an entire series about a burglar named Bernie who owns a used bookstore. Bernie's bookstore attracts a shocking number of corrupt cops, murderers, criminals, and other assorted riff-raff, and it doesn't earn Bernie much money, but it's a nice place to rest and read between burgling and solving murders. I suppose your opinion of used bookstores mostly depends on your outlook, and Orwell was something of a negative Nellie.

Back in Normalcy there was precisely one used bookstore. Like most used bookstores, it was located in a neighborhood that was slightly scruffy. It was called Lowry's Books, and the store's proprietor, who I always assumed was Lowry himself, was an ancient man. He was nearly seven feet tall, a gaunt, cadaverous creature, with a thick tuft of white hair on top of his head and skin of a translucent whiteness. From my junior through my senior years in high school I went to his bookstore at least three times a week, and every time I opened the door I would be greeted the same way, "Hello. Have you ever been here before? The science fiction books are over there."

A more sensitive young man than myself would have taken offense at his obstinate refusal to remember my face. I was also tempted to be offended that he assumed that because I was a teenager I wanted to read science fiction. He didn't know what my tastes were! I could have been there to purchase a complete set of À *la recherche du temps perdu* in the original French!

But I wasn't ever there to buy a complete set of *À la recherche du temps perdu*, so I let it go.

It was a bad idea to go into Lowry's Books looking for a specific book. You had to go in with an open mind and just browse, allowing the spirit of the place to guide you. You had to run your fingers along the spines, read titles, look at the names of authors, and hope to find something that would tempt you to pull a volume from the shelf. This was the only way to approach Lowry's Books because, for one thing, the old man probably didn't have the book you wanted, and for another, even if he did have it, it wouldn't be tucked away on the shelves in any kind of order; you had to stumble into it by accident. Books were packed into various zones of the bookstore according to genre, but there was no attempt to organize them beyond that and the borders between the genre zones were amorphous and blurry. Lowry couldn't be bothered with anything like alphabetization.

I once saw a picture of a bookstore in London that had been hit by a bomb during the Blitz. In the photograph, the front wall of the store has been blown away, books are scattered everywhere, and a young man is sitting amid the debris. He is reading a damaged book, oblivious to the world. That was me at Lowry's Books. Book in hand, surrounded by a disorganized chaos of books, and absorbed completely by the neatly ordered words in front of my eyes.

Eventually, old Lowry disappeared and was replaced by his son. The younger Lowry remodeled the shop, tearing out its horrible carpet with its coffee stains and funky smell and leaving bare wood floors. He installed more and brighter lights. He sorted the jumbled piles of undifferentiated reading material and alphabetized everything. If you are looking for a specific book now you can ask the younger Lowry if they have it and after 10 seconds of tapping at his computer he will have an answer for you. Not only that, if the book is in stock, he will be able to tell you where in the store you can find it, and he may even walk you over to it himself. I've been told they do most of their business online, through Amazon. It's terribly depressing. Whenever I visit my parents in Normalcy I drop by. Lowry Junior recognizes me and calls me "Elvis" because I bought an Elvis Cole mystery from him right after he took the place over. I browse around for a while, usually I buy something, but it just isn't the same.

Now that I've decided to write a novel, used bookshops have become menacing places. Their walls are fifteen feet high and the books on the top shelves look down on me like gods in judgment. "So, you think your progeny will be worthy to join us?" they seem to sneer. Ah, but I don't need to worry about those books up on the top shelf, nobody will ever buy them anyway. Nobody can read their spines, and who wants to climb that rickety old ladder to inspect them? They're just bookstore ballast and can sneer at me all they want.

I had to find ways to fill my hours now that I wasn't working or watching television at home, so despite my discomfort I decided to step into a small used bookshop on Polk. The clerk glanced up at me as I walked in, but his face immediately went back down to his computer. I passed the counter and headed back towards the fiction section where I planned to look at the wall of novels. One of them caught my eye and I pull it down from its shelf. It was a copy of *A Journal of the Plague Year*. Would I buy it? Maybe. I still had a bit of money after all. But I was in no hurry and my selection process involves a series of steps:

1. **Ask myself what I know about the book.** Has anyone recommended it to me? Have people talked to me about it? In this case, no and no.

2. **Inspect the front cover.** Of course, we have all been warned by that ancient platitude that we should "never judge a book by its cover." But this is nonsense. The cover has a lot of useful information on it. The author's name for example. In this case that name was Daniel Defoe, who I knew had written Robinson Crusoe, a famous and well-regarded book that I had neither read nor particularly wanted to read. I could also see that this was a Penguin edition. I prefer the cheap mass market Bantam editions of these old public domain books, but I had to admit that the cover of the Penguin edition was handsome. It had a woodcut of death, in the shape of a skeleton, menacing London with a spear. I liked it.

3. **Inspect the back cover.** Once again, that rule of "never judge a book by its cover" is proved ridiculous. The back of the book has the section describing what the book is about, and how is a reader supposed to decide whether he wants to read a book or not without taking a look at that? In this case, the back cover said, "In 1665 the plague swept through London, claiming over 97,000 lives. Daniel Defoe was just five at the time of the plague, but he later called on his own memories, as well as his writing experience, to create this vivid chronicle of the epidemic and its victims. *A Journal* (1722) follows Defoe's fictional narrator as he traces the devastating progress of the plague through the streets of

London. Here we see a city transformed: some of its streets suspiciously empty, some - with crosses on their doors - overwhelmingly full of the sounds and smells of human suffering. And every living citizen he meets has a horrifying story that demands to be heard." I don't know how many useful memories a person can carry from the age of five all the way into adulthood, but still, it sounded like a Restoration version of the movie *Contagion*. It sounded good.

4.**Blurbs.** Blurbs are suspect, but still helpful. A publisher can always find somebody to say something nice about pretty much anything. Every book has its blurbs and I don't think it's possible to find a horror novel that Stephen King hasn't said something nice about. In this case, Penguin found a quote by Anthony Burgess and another one by the historian Peter Ackroyd. Those two guys liked it, maybe I would too?

5.**Read a bit of the book.** I once bought a book because it had been recommended to me, I liked the cover, it had good blurbs, and the synopsis sounded interesting. But when I got home and read the first paragraph (which had been written in the present tense) I knew I had made a mistake, and though I suffered through another thirty pages or so, I abandoned it in the end, not caring a tuppence for what happened to any of its characters. But in the case of A Journal of the Plague Year, I liked what I read. It was written in 17-something-or-other, which gave it an archaically tangy vocabulary, but it was easy to read and the subject was an interesting one to me.

6.**Flip through the pages.** Sharp readers will remember that in Chapter 3 I splattered orange sauce on pages 317-326 of *The Nix,* and I have learned through sad experience that many readers whose books find their way into used bookstores are even bigger slobs than I am. Sometimes you find nice things tucked away in the pages of a book. I have found bookmarks, leaves, photographs, dollar bills, and the stubs of concert tickets in the pages of used books. I like these artifacts left by previous readers. Remember (also from Chapter 3, that essential chapter) that a book is a bridge between people, and sometimes it can be a sort of bridge between people who will never even meet. But I have also found ketchup, blood, torn pages, boogers, idiotic margin notes, and hair tucked away between the pages. I like to make sure there are no nasty surprises hiding between the covers of a book before I buy it. I flipped through *A Journal of the Plague Year* and I found a couple pieces of folded paper, but no blood and no dollar bills.

7. **Price.** How can you put a price on literature? With a sticker, usually. This time the sticker said "$4.99". A good deal, but also almost all the rest of my money.

As I was running *A Journal of the Plague Year* through my admissions process, I saw another man enter the fiction aisle that I had until then occupied by myself. He looked nervous, guilty even. When he glanced up at me and noticed I was looking at him he quickly looked away. I thought that he must be a shoplifter, and his nervousness was so evident that it had to be his first time. "Don't do it, buddy, don't do it," I thought in his direction. When I bent my eyes to my book again, I watched him in my peripheral vision. He glanced at me, convinced himself I wasn't looking, and then lifted the front of his shirt and pulled out a book that he'd been carrying in his waistband. He glanced at me again, and again convinced himself I wasn't paying attention, and then he slid the book into place on the shelf. He hurried away and a moment later I heard the bell tinkle as he left the store.

He must have been a repentant book thief, I thought, come to return some book he'd stolen after being afflicted by feelings of guilt. I was curious to discover what book he had stolen and I found it almost immediately. While watching him out of the corner of my eye I had been able to see roughly where he had put it (a middle shelf in the Science Fiction section), and I had also noticed that the cover was a distinctively clean and shiny shade of baby blue that stuck out like a broken tooth in this store full of greasy, crumpled books with foxed pages and battered spines.

I pulled the book out of the stack and inspected the cover. "*Moon War*, By Thomas Crawley", it said. It was clearly a self-published book, printed on cheap paper and cut at an off center slant. Flipping through the pages I noticed formatting issues and a few typos. There was no ISBN number on the back. No barcode. On the inside cover somebody had written in pencil "New $8.00". And suddenly I realized that the person I had taken for a shoplifter was actually the author of this book, Mr. Thomas Crawley himself, come to slip his book among the volumes that had been published by proper publishers after having been edited by proper editors and represented by proper literary agents.

And I could clearly imagine Mr. Crawley in his small apartment. I could see him getting the idea for the novel, telling his friends about the plot, characters, and futuristic world he had created in his mind. I could see him sitting down in the glow of his laptop late at night, typing quietly so as not to awaken his wife who had work in the morning. He had work in the morning as well, but writing, he knew, was his real work. He typed month after month, battling through bouts of doubt, writer's block, and self-hatred, trying to get that word count up to 60,000 so he could tell people he had written a novel. I could see his pride upon finishing it. I could see him sharing the manuscript with trusted friends, and the smile on his face when they responded with positive words. I could see him polishing it to an opaline shine and then sending it off into the world. The first rejection letter was a blow, but not too hard. He hadn't expected a smooth path. I could see the thirteenth rejection letter, and the fourteenth, and the fifteenth. I watched each one of those self-addressed stamped envelopes land with a hollow thud at the bottom of his mailbox like a slap to his face. At first, he approached these letters with hope. Hope was soon replaced by dread, then resignation. Finally, after fifty rejections and not a single encouraging word from anybody whose opinion mattered, he turned to self-publishing. The coward's way out. And here it was, the result of all that labor. He had placed it in a bookstore without that store's permission because at this point he had abandoned any hope of fame or fortune, and he just wanted someone to read his book. Just once! Just one reader who wasn't his sister or his dad or his friend! He had placed his book in the stacks and abandoned it in the hope it would somehow find that reader. I had just witnessed an act akin to Jochebed setting Moses adrift on the Nile.

How could I not be moved by this?

Should I buy the book? I wondered

I submitted it to my test:

1. **Ask myself what I knew about the book.** Its creation was an act of love and devotion.

2. **Inspect the front cover.** It was a public domain picture of the moon, with the title and the author's name written in Copperplate Gothic across it.

3. **Inspect the back cover.** Just a wall of blue.

4. **Blurbs.** None.

5. **Read a bit of the book.** "The year was 2233 and nukes were about to rain down on the moon like rain in a rainstorm. Commander Zarta's boobs, which had grown to an enormous size due to the low gravity on the moon, jiggled

sexily as she flew her space raptor to intercept the lethal cones of death." I groaned. I had really been hoping against hope to find a gem. I had been hoping to cry out, "Why, Thomas Crawley, you genius! Those agents! Those publishers! What fools!" But after two sentences it was perfectly clear that the naysayers been right. One of the worst things about this planet is that the naysayers are almost always right.

6. **Flip through.** Nothing but clean, crisp pages.
7. **Price.** "$8.00"

In this great country where everyone thinks he has a novel in him, this same sad drama is being played out, in slightly different ways, again and again and again. It is an endless roller coaster of hope, failure, and desperation.

I slid *Moon War* back into its place on the shelf. No doubt it would sit there for months before being noticed by an employee of the bookstore and tossed into the garbage. Hopefully, Thomas Crawley would interpret its disappearance from the shelves to mean that it had been bought and read. Maybe he would convince himself that the reader had enjoyed it.

As for me, I bought my copy of *A Journal of the Plague Year* and set out to find a place to read it.

Chapter 9

I wandered over to Van Ness and sat in the doorway of a
failed dry cleaners. That's what the homeless do; they sit in
doorways. After a few minutes I decided to spend the night
there. I condemned myself for my cowardice of the night
before. Thousands of people sleep in the streets every night.
If lunatics and crack addicts could do it, so could I. Having
come to this resolution I spent another hour searching in
dumpsters for cardboard to use as mattress material and I
recovered several relatively clean boxes and even an old
couch cushion. But after sitting on the couch cushion for a
while I realized that it didn't smell right, and I had to take it
back to the dumpster.

Once I got settled in, I pulled out my copy of *A Journal
of the Plague Year*. I had spent my last few dollars to buy it,
but they were well spent. It was every bit as good as I could
have hoped, and I read half of it as the hours passed and
night got closer. After I'd gotten my fill of reading, I closed
the book and was admiring its cover when I remembered the
loose sheets of paper I had noticed tucked into its pages
earlier. I pulled them out and studied them. They were
written in cursive, in a feminine hand, and I read:

*If you had asked either of them, both Edward Morgan
and Jeremiah Cooper would have told you that he was a
member of the Church of England in good standing. If you
had asked the vicar at Saint Mary's where their Sunday
observance was somewhat irregular, he would not have been
so certain. The vicar had weighed both of them in matters of
religion and had found them equally wanting. Morgan
considered himself a natural philosopher, and the vicar
feared that perhaps his studies had led him away to a mental*

condition perilously close to atheism. Cooper, on the other hand, was very religious, but the vicar feared that his fervent devotions may have swept him beyond the gospel as laid down by the Church, and into dark realms of superstition.

If you had asked Edward Morgan if Jeremiah Cooper was his friend, he would have denied it with a fervor bordering on anger, and if you had asked Jeremiah Cooper about his friendship with Edward Morgan, you would have received a very similar reaction. And yet the people who knew the two of them, and indeed there were very few who knew the one without knowing the other, thought of them as a pair. For, despite their avowed detestation of one another they were held together as if by a kind of personal gravity that would never permit one of them to escape his orbit of the other.

They lived side by side in a narrow alley near Aldgate, and their houses were very similar in appearance. Each owned a home that was three stories tall. Three stories may sound like a lot, but their homes were so narrow that despite the abundance of stories there was a scarcity of square footage. Morgan's house had a parlor in front and a small kitchen in back on the first floor, a dining room in front and his bedroom in back on the second, and servants quarters and his study on the third. All of these rooms were small and cramped. Cooper's home was filled with different furniture and had a different master but was otherwise nearly identical.

The two homes had originally been built two inches apart, but they had been built ninety years earlier and the intervening decades had been hard on them. The snow, ice, wind, rain and sun had gradually pushed them into each other so that now their third floors snuggled close together and not a ray of sunlight could pass between them. This contact between their homes was a recurring flashpoint *between Morgan and Cooper, each blaming the home of the other for the contact, and each imagining that this contact was causing damage to his own house. In fact, each house was leaning into the other at roughly the same angle, and if you had removed either one of them, the other would have instantly toppled over.*

There were some things that they could agree on. They had both been born and raised during the reign of Good Queen Bess, and they agreed with a burning ardor that would accept no counter argument, she was the greatest monarch seen in England since Edward III. They had also each been supporters of the monarchy through the barbaric protectorate of Oliver Cromwell, and they had been ecstatic upon the restoration of Charles II, but subsequently disappointed by the man himself.

In fact, the two avowed enemies agreed on a great many things, but each of them found himself annoyed at the grounds upon which the other based his opinion. They agreed, for example, that the execution of Charles I had been a dreadful crime. Morgan believed this to be so because it was his opinion that the sentence had been illegal, and he was annoyed to hear Cooper go on and on about how God reigned over mankind as king, and had therefore established kingship as the perfect mode of government, and to kill the king of England, the likeness of God on Earth, was to commit a barbaric act of blasphemy. The result of their discussions of the topic was that even though they agreed with one another, each was heartily irritated at the other.

And yet, despite not being friends, and, in fact, claiming to be enemies, they spent a great deal of time together. One reason for this apparent paradox was the fact that each of them enjoyed argument, and each man found a perfect sparring partner in the other. They were also both old men, well into their sixth decades of life, and their wives and

67

children had died before them. Argument, proximity, age, and loneliness had pushed them together like their old houses, whether they liked it or not. And removing one would have likely destroyed the other.

When, in the early spring of 1665 rumors of the plague began to pick up again, the two spoke to each other upon the subject many times. There was a routine to these conversations, and each night for five or six weeks they engaged in a remarkably similar dialogue on the subject of the coming plague. Morgan was not bothered by the fact that Cooper always repeated the same things that he had said before, because Morgan intended to repeat his own lines as well. Only occasionally, when something interesting had happened on a particular day, would that event be folded into the general pattern of conversation. The dialogue would remain otherwise unchanged.

"I told you, didn't I? I told you when we saw that comet pass last year that a terrible calamity was on the way."

"Indeed you did," conceded Morgan, "but it was I who said that this portended calamity would be a plague, and now we see that London is falling prey to a hideous distemper, and that I was correct."

"Bah. I also knew it would be a distemper that God would inflict upon us. A comet is a warning from Providence. A sign that He intends to chasten us."

"Nonsense! A comet is no such thing! Men of a philosophic mold know well that comets pass by design, and like the planets they make their circuit around the sun in a determined order. God set the comets in motion as he did the planets. And how can a comet be a warning when it passes at an assigned time according to a foreordained pattern? A comet is no messenger from the Lord, it is merely an astral

68

body making its way through the heavens, although the Lord set it in its original path."

They were having this conversation, as they had many of their conversations, as each stood on the roof of his respective house, for each of them had, some fifteen years earlier, constructed a platform, a deck as wide as the house and about ten feet deep on top of his house. Morgan used this space for his celestial observations, for he had purchased a telescope at considerable expense, and it was his most prized possession. Cooper used his space for growing herbs, and his deck was green and cluttered with potted plants that were said to possess magical medicinal qualities. But mostly, each of them used this space on the top of his house as a place where he could go and argue with his neighbor.

Morgan continued, "Comets are well known to emit an effluvium of noxious gasses as they trail through the sky. Yay, the tail of the comet is itself nothing but the visible manifestation of these harmful vapors. I can assure you that this comet was no messenger bearing witness of the coming plague, it brought the plague itself. And it did so through natural causes, not by the command of a vengeful God."

"Heresy! Heresy! It is a terrible heresy to deny the visitation of God when it has so clearly been made manifest! Beware lest you fall victim to this distemper like the Israelites of old who did not look to the sign of the snake raised up by Moses when they were stricken down by disease and disbelief!"

The pair could have gone back and forth for some time with this recurring dispute between determinism and deism, but there had been new events that day, and Morgan decided to fold them into the discussion. "They say that Old Tom Biggins was taken by the plague yesterday."

69

"Who is this 'they' that you speak of? I saw Tom not three days ago and he looked well enough to wrestle a plow horse, and to pin it too."

"Yes, but it came upon him suddenly, like the angel of death that visited the Egyptians in the days of Moses, taking the firstborn sons of Egypt, all of them, in the space of one night."

Cooper was always receptive of arguments based in the Bible, particularly the Old Testament, and this comparison made him pause and reflect. "Like the angel of death" he repeated in a tone of awe.

And that was the end of the writing.

I knew what I was looking at. This was somebody's abandoned novel. They had read *A Journal of the Plague Year* and in a flash of inspiration they started writing a story set during the plague. They hadn't finished it. They would never finish it now. It was a shame too, because I liked both Cooper and Morgan and I wanted to know what would happen to them. Would they both survive? Would they both die? Would Cooper die and Morgan finally realize how much he had loved his enemy?

I wondered how many unfinished books exist in the universe. For every book you see on the shelves of a library there must be dozens, hundreds, maybe thousands that were started and abandoned, left like imperfect babies on a Spartan hillside. The problem is that people think writing fiction is a flash of inspiration and it isn't. It's long hard work. It's like bricklaying but with words. One on top of the next, for hour upon hour, with each word carrying a moral, intellectual, comic, or aesthetic weight instead of a physical one.

What I was holding in my hands was somebody's flash of inspiration, a flash that wasn't supported by a willingness to do drudge work.

Chapter 10

The first night I tried to sleep in the streets of San Francisco was even worse than my night I had spent in the Marin Headlands. The air was a little warmer, my doorway provided some shelter from the wind, and my bed of cardboard was more comfortable than the rocks of the previous night, but these improvements were overwhelmed by a battalion of negative factors. Van Ness is a busy street and cars, motorcycles, busses, trucks, and pedestrians passed noisily by without intermission. It's hard to let your guard down and allow yourself to sleep on the streets. Thoughts of roving bands of cruel teens, cops wielding truncheons, and murderous vagrants intent on stealing my last dollar filled my brain and destroyed any chance of sleep. I knew that if I drifted off even for a moment I would be awakened by a blow from a baseball bat wielded by a soulless youth out to kill someone (like that man in Folsom Prison) just to watch him die.

Finally, at around two or three in the morning, I did manage to sleep for perhaps an hour. I was simply overcome by exhaustion. I dropped my guard and drifted uneasily into unconsciousness. I was torn from this feeble rest when some punk on a motorcycle went screaming through an intersection as a light turned green. Though I remained on my back for a few more hours I could not fall asleep again. I watched people and cars pass by from the perspective of the pavement. When the sun at last began to rise I found an open café where I ordered a cup of coffee with my very last dollar. I added much more cream and sugar to it than usual, figuring that I had better get my money's worth.

I walked to the Alta Plaza in Pacific Heights to take a nap and I found a sort of perverse pleasure in being a bum in a neighborhood where the streets are walled with multimillion dollar homes. I'm poking a stick in the eyeball of all the snobs that live here, and it gives me an odd kick. All those old Victorian mansions seemed to be glaring at me with disapproval as I penetrated Pacific Heights.

I found a spot in a quiet corner of the park where I soon dozed off. It was a pleasant sort of sleep, the relaxing kind that erases tension and reanimates the flesh. If I had been allowed fifteen more minutes of it, I would have classified the day as an unqualified success. Unfortunately, as I dozed a drop of water formed in a cloud a few thousand feet above me. It was a large, cold drop of water and when it fell towards the earth it quickly gathered momentum. It must have been going about 90 mph when it hit me squarely on my closed eyelid like the slap of an angry woman. I was immediately awake. A moment later a levee broke in the sky and water came gushing down like it hasn't since the days of Noah. I had to run for cover.

There was nowhere to go. I sprinted down the street in search of a shelter of some kind, but I was in a residential neighborhood and couldn't very well ensconce myself on somebody's porch. I ran towards Van Ness where I found cover in the doorway of a closed bank. There was a homeless man there already, but he was sleeping and didn't notice my arrival. I sat as far away from him as I could, and I commenced shivering.

Chapter 11

It rained the entire afternoon and I was stuck in the doorway of a closed bank with an awful smelling man whose name, I eventually discovered, was Rick. The bank's entryway was spacious, at least fifteen feet across with no fewer than six glass doors (none of which had been opened in quite some time). My companion was apparently sleeping one off and had a small mound of empty bottles of cheap vodka piled up near his head. The smell coming from him was perniciously pungent. Even with the wind infusing our shelter with fresh air there was no way to escape his decayed odor. It was so bad that I would have thought he was dead and had been rotting for several days if it hadn't been for the occasional grunts that came from his crumpled form.

I wrote in my journal until my hand began to cramp and I had to stop. Once I was done writing I tried to think of a way to pass the time. I had no television, I had no phone, and I had no hobbies to work on. I had nothing to do except sit there and contemplate my companion.

He was wearing stained underpants over his head. They were pulled down so far that no part of his face could be seen. The underpants were white jockey shorts with the letters BVD imprinted on the waistband. When I say "white," I am using the word in the loosest possible sense. In fact, they reminded me of the old joke about the guy who goes to the doctor's office for a checkup and the doctor tells him "I'm going to need a stool sample and a urine sample." The guy pauses for a moment before answering, "Okay, but I'm in a hurry; can I just leave my underwear?" I say "white" because the BVDs had no doubt at one point been white, but they were now covered with a patchwork of stains in various shades of yellow and brown.

How did these underpants get onto his head, I wondered? Had he placed them there himself to keep his face warm? It was cold after all. Or had they been placed there by some malevolent prankster who thought the sight of dirty underpants on a poor man's head would be funny?

The man was inserted into a gray sleeping bag that had been scarred by a multitude of rips. White stuffing was oozing out of these tears like pus from infected wounds. There were several sheets of cardboard piled up underneath the sleeping bag to help cushion the man's tabernacle of flesh from the harsh spinning surface of the earth, and his head was resting on a folded copy of USA Today. The newsprint smudged the dirty underwear, adding black to the shades of yellow and brown whenever he moved his head in his sleep.

A parade of fellow citizens passed us by. They had their umbrellas out and were hurrying on their way to wherever it was they were going. They didn't want to be out in this weather any longer than necessary. The wind tried to steal their umbrellas. I saw one slender young woman almost pull a Mary Poppins when a particularly powerful gust pushed itself underneath her umbrella and threatened to lift her from the ground. She was pulled onto the tips of her toes before her umbrella was blown inside out and her heels eased back down to the wet pavement. She glanced at me with a nervous smile on her face and then scampered away.

For hours I watched these people go by, hurrying on the manifold errands of their lives. They had work to do, families to return to. I thought of Abigail. I wondered if she liked storms. It was easy to imagine her making a cup of cocoa and sitting in front of the window with a blanket wrapped around her legs. I was sure that she would read Jane Austen and peek up from the pages from time to time to watch the wind toss the mangy heads of the trees lining the street below. She would look beautiful as she read, and her loveliness would only be enhanced in those moments when Austen's wit made her smile. I, on the other hand, had always hated bad weather. When it rained, I would sulk, watch old noir movies, and make semiserious plans to move to Los Angeles.

As I was thinking these things, I noticed some sheets of paper sticking out from underneath the homeless man's cardboard. It was a manuscript. Even he was working on a novel.

I shuffled over to the manuscript and pulled it out as carefully as I could, wanting neither to wake the man nor to damage his work. There were about 300 sheets of loose college ruled paper. The handwriting that covered this paper was surprisingly clear. I flipped through the pages and it looked like the manuscript had been written with at least a dozen different writing implements. I paused for a moment and wondered if it was right to read this man's work. Authors can be very protective of their unfinished projects, not wanting anyone to see their writing until it has achieved their envisioned level of perfection. But as I glanced down at the author of this particular manuscript, with those disgusting underwear pulled over his head, it occurred to me that he probably didn't have a lot of ego left to protect. So, I settled back into my corner and began to read:

The rifts opened, or so I have been told, soon after I was born. Before that it was a golden time. Before the rifts there was an animal called a giraffe. These were big animals with spots and very long necks. Their necks were long, long enough to reach the tops of the trees. Only giraffes could eat leaves so high off the ground. They only lived in Africa and at places called "zoos." A zoo was like a museum, but for living animals.

76

There are no giraffes now. The scientists said that the problem was that giraffes were too tall. Their heads were like lofty towers of Babel trying to reach to heaven. But instead of heaven, all the giraffes found up there was poison gases.

It wasn't humans who did it. I have been told that we thought that we were killing the Earth even before the rifts opened up. People were worried that they were destroying the planet with the way that they lived. Burning gas, shedding plastic like dandruff on a black sweater, chopping down all the forests. Chop. Chop. Chop. Everyone knew that they were doing wrong, and they all said that they wanted to do right, but selfishness is always there. It's hard to do the right thing when the blame for the wrong can be spread over so many people.

I skipped ahead about fifty pages.

Even though there were no giraffes. There were still picture books that had pictures of giraffes. The giraffes always looked so happy in these books, with their heads reaching all the way up to the tops of the trees where the tastiest leaves were. The leaves up there were so tender and smooth. No giraffe would ever eat the lower leaves, because they knew they weren't as sweet...

I skipped ahead another 100 pages:

When a baby giraffe was born it was so cute. They would try to stand on their rickety legs. One time, at the zoo, when he was a kid, the man had seen a baby giraffe. He was there at the zoo with his dad and it was special because even back in the days when giraffes were around, a new giraffe wasn't born every day. He and his dad, and a crowd of

77

*other people, all watched as this baby giraffe tried to get up
again and again. His legs wobbled and he tumbled down
like a Tinker Toy statue. The man (who was a boy then)
wanted to stay until the baby giraffe finally found a way to
stand, but his father took a last drink from the bottle in his
bag and said that it was time to go. He never got to see that
baby giraffe stand. And now they were all dead. All of them.
All the giraffes were dead. Some hadn't even been buried.
They just collapsed and rotted where they were.*

I skipped ahead a few more times, reading snatches here
and there, but it was all dead giraffes for pages and pages.
As the semi dark of a rainy day slipped towards the full
darkness of night, my companion began to stir and I
hurriedly crammed his manuscript back under his cardboard.
It turned out there hadn't been any need to be in such a hurry
about it. The process waking up was long and apparently
quite painful. First, he began to mumble in his sleep, "oh no,
oh no, oh no, oh no . . ." He mumbled just those two words,
over and over again. Next, he began to scream. All day
long people had been walking by the two of us, pretending
not to notice that we existed. This had been an effortless
endeavor on their part. Ignoring the homeless is second
nature to any urbanite, and they strolled past us unperturbed.
This became much more difficult for them now that there
was a man with underwear pulled over his head screaming
out curses. He yelled as if he was suffering the purgatorial
penalty of the most sinful man on earth. People still walked
by pretending there was nothing going on, but with
stiffening faces and sidelong glances I could see that my
companion's tortured noises were having an effect.

At last, when I could take no more of the miserable
cacophony and was about to run out into the storm to escape,
the man stopped. His screaming ended abruptly and was

78

replaced by pathetic whimpering. He whimpered for at least an hour before he stopped and coughed. The coughing apparently hurt because it was cut short and a sorrowful moan took its place, "ooooowwwwwwww." Then, finally, I heard conscious words spoken.

"What the hell?"

His hands came up to the underpants and he repeated the question. He pulled them off his head. "What in the . . .?" He sat up and looked at me with a deep scowl etched in the dirty creases of his weathered face.

"Hello," I said as pleasantly as I could.

He had no time for pleasantries. "You put these . . .these . . . dirty man-panties on my head?"

"No."

He eyed me suspiciously, trying to decide whether to believe me or not. "Did you see who did it?"

"No, they were on when I got here."

"How long ago was that?"

"I'm not sure. Six hours?"

He was appalled, "You mean I've had these things on my head for six hours?"

"At least. There's really no way to know how long they were on before I got here."

"And you don't know who did it?"

"No."

"Well somebody did it."

"Yeah."

"Underwears don't just put themselves on people's heads."

"Not in my experience, no."

He took a moment to scrutinize the underpants that had been on his head and reconsidered his last statement, "I guess these ones might have. It ain't a stretch to imagine these things crawling around under their own power."

79

"Are they yours?" I asked.

My question made him rummage in his pants for a moment before replying, "No. and I don't know if it would be better or worse if they had been mine."

I made no reply.

He turned to me, "Hey, you got anything to drink?"

"No."

"You wouldn't hold out on me, would you? I need it for medicinal purposes."

"Sorry, I don't have a drop on me."

He rummaged through his pile of empty bottles before finding one that had about just enough medicine to fill a teaspoon. He sucked it down.

"That just makes me thirstier." He looked at me again, "Do you have anything to smoke?"

"No."

"You sure?"

"Yep."

"You ain't holding out on me, are you?"

"Nope."

"After all, I am sharing my humble abode with you ain't I?"

"Yes, thank you."

He eyed me suspiciously again before rummaging about in his sleeping bag and pulling out a crumpled package of cigarettes. He shook out one pathetically bent and bedraggled white cylinder and put it up to his chapped mouth. He lit it with a match from a book that he kept tucked into the pack. "You want a drag?" he asked with flaky lips.

"No thanks."

He seemed relieved by my answer. "What an ugly day."

I agreed.

With the ice broken we chatted for a while. He told me his name was Rick and he was from Hayward. He had been a longshoreman but was fired for being an alcoholic, which, he insisted, was not the case, at least not at the time. He did most of the talking and I did most of the listening. He seemed to enjoy having someone to speak to and after several days of near silence I was content to listen.

He told me about his book, of course. It was a cautionary tale about a man living in a giraffeless post-apocalyptic wasteland. I tried to pretend that I didn't know all about it. He grew increasingly amiable as I made positive comments about his giraffe novel and after a while he even offered me one of his sheets of cardboard.

"Oh no," I protested, "I don't want to take your cardboard." He insisted, however, and got out of his sleeping bag long enough to pick up a piece of cardboard and carry it to me. He had to pause for a moment on his way over to lean against the glass doors of the bank. "Oh, no, oooooh no," he moaned. When he was close the smell was almost overpowering and it took every ounce of my self-possession to keep from gagging. I accepted the cardboard with thanks.

The ten foot walk from his bed to my side of the doorway seemed to have taken a lot out of him, and he lay back down immediately upon returning to his nest. After that he spoke very little. He just stared at the doors of the bank, apparently lost in his own thoughts. Finally, I fell asleep. I think I must have felt some comfort in Rick's presence that allowed me to lower my guard so that I could rest. I had by far my best night of sleep since I left home a few days ago and I awoke this morning feeling fully rested. Rick was gone when I awoke, but his pile of bottles remained. It was cold and cloudy, but the rain had stopped.

I was very hungry. I only had a few cents and I hadn't eaten anything since the previous day. I was either going to have to start begging, or starve.

Chapter 12

After I left the shelter of the bank entryway where I had spent the night, I walked down the hill (with a piece of cardboard under my arm) and began to look for a good place to panhandle. I wanted a prime location that saw lots of foot traffic but had not yet been claimed by anyone else. There are, after all, a lot of bums in this city, and panhandling space, as much as residential or office space, is at a premium. I found a promising location on the corner of Van Ness and Sutter and sat there with my back against the wall of an electronics store. The felt of my marker rested against the cardboard, but I didn't write. I had planned to make a sign because it seemed less frightening than the alternative. I simply could not see myself walking up to strangers and directly asking them, "Could you give me a dollar?" With a sign to make the embarrassing request for me I could just put a cup on the ground, hang my head, and allow generosity to take its course.

I decided to make my plea simple and direct: "I'm very hungry, please help." I wrote these words across the face of my cardboard strip before pointing it towards the street, placing a cup on the ground, and waiting. The cup was paper, and it kept tipping over in the breeze. People walked by. Most ignored me. The panhandling market is saturated and it's hard for a newcomer to break into the industry. Nevertheless, after about fifteen minutes a young couple stopped in front of me and asked how to get to "the curviest street in the world." It was clear from the look of them that they were on their honeymoon. They were very young and very attractive. The girl seemed a little afraid of me, and this evident fear inflicted a small but inescapable twinge of pain on me. She held onto her man's arm and stood a half a step behind him. Like a nervous faun, she appeared ready to bolt at the slightest unanticipated noise. I told them it was too far to walk and gave the number of the proper bus while suggesting that Uber would be the easiest way to get there. They said, "thank you" and the young man gave me a wadded up one dollar bill which he had been keeping in his front pant pocket. The bill was still warm from being pressed against his thigh, but the warmth quickly dissipated in the breeze. I could tell by looking at him that he was the sort of person who withheld money from beggars on principle, but he made an exception in this case because I had provided a sort of service.

It seemed odd that the girl had been afraid of me. No one had ever been afraid of me before and I don't like it. Some people get a kick out of being scary, and when they walk down the street they like to see the crowd part before them like the waters of Jordan before the bearers of the ark. They get jobs as elementary school principals or highway patrol officers. I am not that type of person. Usually I just want to go unnoticed.

I don't know how long I sat at that street corner. It was probably no more than two hours, but my hunger lengthened the minutes. At the end of it I had seven dollars and twenty-seven cents, and I immediately went looking for a place to spend my meager earnings on food. The closest likely place was a dingy looking café on Polk. I almost bolted from the premises, however, when a Vietnamese girl asked me where I would like to be seated. *Be seated*? I thought to myself, *I don't know if I can afford to eat any place where I have to 'be seated.'* But I sat down anyway and read the menu with an eye for prices. I saw that the lunch special was an egg salad sandwich, pickle wedge, and French fries for six dollars and seventy-five cents. When the girl returned, I gave her my order. She smiled and said that she would be back with it in just a moment.

"Uh, and one more thing," I said apologetically, "I'm afraid that I'm not going to be able to give you much of a tip, uh, so go ahead and give me lousy service if you want to."

She laughed pleasantly and returned to the kitchen.

The waitress didn't fear me at all apparently, and she didn't even seem miffed that a customer had just admitted that he planned to stiff her when it came to the tip. Was I experiencing actual human kindness? I almost felt happy for a moment, but then I realized that though the waitress did not see me as a frightening person, she saw me as something much worse: a pitiful person. It was alright if I didn't give her a tip; it wasn't expected of me. Who was I to be tipping people anyway?

I was hungrier than I had ever been before. My stomach had been grumbling since the afternoon of the previous day. A slight growl is as far into starvation as most people in the United States ever get. I was way past the quiet growl by now. I had actual pain in my belly. My stomach, that ugly, tentacled, acidic, selfish monster, had begun to gnaw on itself. I felt weak and light-headed. Every one of my muscles seemed to be crying out for some kind of nourishment, and the food was taking too long to get to my table. It wasn't helpful to reflect that there are literally millions of people on the planet who feel this way almost all the time.

I had picked the egg salad sandwich because of its price but I had also assumed that it would be something that the cook could throw together quickly. I hadn't factored in the time it would take to make the French fries.

At last the waitress brought out a thick white plate with food piled high upon it. I ate the pickle wedge first to get it out of the way. Next, I dumped ketchup all over my fries and devoured them like an aardvark ravaging an anthill. As my tongue flickered the fries disappeared. They were still too hot and they burned the roof of my mouth, but in the madness of my feeding frenzy I hardly noticed. The most important thing was getting them into my stomach as quickly as possible. Finally, I turned to the sandwich. The French fries had partially pacified my hunger, so I slowed down to enjoy the egg salad. I took every bite with great deliberation. I chewed very slowly, savoring the taste of eggs, onions, mayonnaise and sweet pickle relish. I enjoyed the way that every single swallow made me feel a bit fuller than I had felt before.

As soon as I swallowed the last inch of crust I was surprised by a sense of remorse. I had just spent almost all my money, almost all that precious store of coins that had been accumulated through the humiliation that is begging. I would be left with a quarter at most when tax was factored into my bill. I felt like the decent man who has just consummated an adulterous relationship. Now the lust that had fueled sin had been quenched and I could no longer remember what had driven me to do something so repugnant to my sense of moral responsibility. The sandwich had been consumed, and all that was left was regret. Before the waitress could return to me with the bill, I took out all of my money and dumped it on the table. There were two crumpled one-dollar bills and a molehill of change. The sight of this meager mound made me instantly become aware of how pitiful my life had become. I fled the café.

I now had no choice but to take up my sign once more and cast myself upon the mercy of the faceless mob. There was a difference in me now though. The taboo against

85

panhandling had been smashed. I even went to far as to start asking people for money, at least those with kind faces, and by the end of the day I had pulled in an additional twenty dollars.

Chapter 13

Interstate 80 flows out of the East Coast beginning at a place called Teaneck, New Jersey. It winds its way through the wooded hills of Pennsylvania and crosses desolate patches of the rust belt before slicing its way through endless miles of corn in Iowa and Nebraska. In the barren sagebrush of Wyoming antelope watch trucks lumber by on I-80's hardtop while they placidly chew the dry grass, and in Nevada wild horses look on from distant mountainsides. Then I-80 struggles its way upward through the Sierra Nevada like the little engine that could before plunging down the other side and into the wide and fruitful expanse of the Sacramento Valley. The interstate weaves its way through yellow hills before descending to sea level, crossing the Bay Bridge, and pouring its guts into San Francisco.

At its far western end, Interstate 80 is elevated to allow local traffic to freely pass back and forth underneath, and as an unintentional side effect it provides shelter for a few dozen members of San Francisco's homeless population. Even before beginning this low rent odyssey I had been aware that the area was a gathering place for the homeless, and I was curious to take a look at it from my new perspective. Maybe it would be a place I could set up camp.

The air was alive with the kinds of gusty microwinds that are pushed into being by moving vehicles. Cars, trucks, and motorcycles roared and honked and beeped and screeched their tires, and though it probably calmed a little at night, it was doubtless loud at all hours. Even worse than the noise, the air was saturated with noxious fumes from the traffic. Oxygen was being remorselessly transformed into carbon monoxide by the malignant magic of the internal combustion engine as I watched. I didn't like any part of it. I thought I would probably be better off going back to the doorway of my defunct bank on Van Ness (which, come to think of it, is far from the quietest street in the city).

As I was leaving the area, I noticed a sort of hut that had been built on a traffic island between two steel pillars that were holding the freeway up. It was about seven feet wide and five feet high, and had been made with identical copies of a white jacketed hardback book that had been stacked like ice blocks and formed into the shape of an igloo. I had never seen anything like it, so I scurried through traffic to take a better look. As I drew closer a face suddenly peered back at me from the arched opening at one end of the structure. There was a maniacal brilliance in the overly bright blue eyes of that dirty face. The unnatural brightness of these eyes distracted from every other feature and it took me a moment to even notice the rest of the man's face. He had a red beard, bedraggled and flecked with unidentifiable debris, and he was wearing a Golden State Warriors beanie that had once been yellow but was now almost black. His smile revealed a nearly complete set of teeth (only one was missing). These teeth were in good order, either the product of quality genetics or expensive orthodontics, but they were slimy and unclean.

"You've come to visit me? Yes? Yes?" he asked.

"No," I corrected him, "I was just passing by and I noticed your interesting little home and I…"

He cut me off, "Come in! Come in! Yes! Yes! You have to come in!"

A couple weeks earlier there was no way I would have followed this deranged man into his hovel, but I reminded myself that this might be something I could write about, so I ducked and followed.

It was dark inside. The structure was under the shade of the interstate and the only light admitted to the interior came from a small oculus in the roof. It was just bright enough for me to see a pile of dirty blankets, a couple empty bottles of malt liquor, and a plastic crate which he insisted I sit upon as the guest. I sat on the crate and he sat on the ground.

"You're here with news about my book? Yes, yes?"

"I'm sorry, but no."

"No? Never say no! Yes. Yes is the word! You aren't from the publisher?"

"No. Sorry."

"Ah. That is too bad."

"You have a publisher? Do you want to tell me about your book? What's it about?" As I asked this question it suddenly occurred to me that the bricks that constituted the walls of this man's home were unsold copies of his book, and I wished I had not asked.

"I spent five years writing it. Slaved over every word. Handpicked each one and placed it with love in exactly the right place. Yes. Yes. With love. I put together sentences. Beautiful ones. Each word in the right order. Yes. Yes. Beauty and sense. Loveliness and meaning. Yes." He paused for a moment, the smile on his face softening into a sort of serenity before hardening again as he continued. "Paragraphs. Nice ones. I made sure each carried an idea to its conclusion. There were metaphors. Similes. Vividly driving points home. Yes. Oh yes."

He twitched as he spoke, his face contorting on the right side, his neck moving his head in little snaps. His tones and twitches alternated between ecstasy and despair as he told his story.

"I wrote a beautiful book. Beautiful. Lovely pages, lovely chapters. Clarity and wit. It could help people. Yes. Really help. I spent thousands on editing. Five thousand. You have to spend money to make money. Yes. Yes, you do. You have to believe in yourself, yes. I believed. I believed. It was going to be a bestseller, yes, it was all

89

arranged, yes. I just had to buy the books, just a few, just to prime the pumps. Yes. Yes! I paid a consultant, thousands, thousands, to make it a bestseller. 'It's all manipulated,' he told me, 'all manipulated to get on the list. And once you make it on the list, you make bank.' Yes! Yes! Bank! He had me buy piles of books. Piles. Piles. This is one house, one, I could have made a city. A whole city. Yes. Yes."

I couldn't follow exactly what had happened, but it was clear that he had been somehow snookered by shady characters operating on the fringes of the publishing industry. Vultures feeding on hope and vanity and despair had torn this man's soul with their ravenous beaks. I felt bad for him.

"I'm sorry," I said, "it sounds like the wrong people got ahold of you."

"Yes. No. I can't be down. Can't be down." A wooden smile was unnaturally forced onto his lips by some source of interior pressure. "I believe. I believe. Things will get better, yes, yes."

"Can I buy a copy of your book?"

"You…" his voice faltered, "You want to read my book?"

"If you would sell me a copy."

"You… you are willing to pay me for a copy?"

"If you can spare one." He rummaged around in the darkness for a moment before drawing out a copy. "It's on sale. You can have it for $10."

I pulled some crumpled bills and a bit of tarnished silver out of my pockets and I handed it to him. He was crying as he handed his book to me. "I hope you like it, yes, yes," he whispered. "This book changed my life. Yes."

I thanked him and crawled out of his igloo of books, glad to be breathing the carbon monoxide outside again, and then I glanced down at the cover.

The cover was dominated by a man's smiling face, and it took me a moment to realize this was the same person I had just met. He was clean shaven on the cover, with his red hair trimmed short and neatly combed. The shine in those blue eyes was there, but it was different. It was a shine of legitimate happiness. Joy even. And his smile was brilliant, clean, and every tooth was present. I learned that his name was Roger Backman, and the title of the books was, *Saying Yes! An Optimist's Guide to Life, Liberty, and the Achievement of Happiness*.

Chapter 14

I was sitting on Hyde street with my back against the wall of a Vietnamese Restaurant. The restaurant had a big green awning that would protect me if it started to rain. I wasn't doing anything, just watching people walk by, waiting for the traffic to quiet down enough so that I could go to sleep. I looked into those haggard Tenderloin faces as they passed. They were of every race; for all its faults the Tenderloin is an incredibly inclusive place. As long as you've hit rock bottom, you are welcome there. It's a magical place where you can get mugged by men and women of every race and religion.

As I started to doze, a man, who had been about to walk by, stopped and looked at me for a moment. Then he leaned his back up against the building about four feet away from me and spoke, "You mind if I smoke?"

"Doesn't bother me. Go ahead."

"Thanks," he pulled a pack of Camels out of the breast pocket of his leather jacket and tapped a white cylinder into his hand. "It's getting so that you can't smoke anywhere anymore. You want one?"

I declined his offer and he sparked up his cigarette with a Zippo. He took a deep pull and then politely blew the smoke away from me. "It's strange that poison can taste so good, that it can feel so necessary to go on living."

I didn't have any addictions, unless you count my overpowering compulsion to remain free of addictions as itself an addiction, but I agreed with him just to stay in character as the world weary old homeless man that I was.

"I've been smoking since I was fourteen. My mom caught me sucking on a cigarette a week or two after I started. She looked at me with disappointment drooping from her face, but she didn't say anything. She just turned

92

the other way. I wish she had slapped it out of my dirty mouth." He gazed into the cloud of smoke he had just exhaled, as if he could still see the memory of it there. "It wouldn't have stopped me though, and she knew it. And I can't stop now either; I need them. I wouldn't be able to write without them. I'm like Kerouac with his bennies. They unlock the words. Of course, if I just smoked while I was writing it would be okay. But I smoke all the time. I walk through life in a cloud."

I liked the look of him as he leaned up against the wall. He seemed so comfortable there, as if for him leaning against a wall was like sitting on a couch for other men. It was obvious that he had lived a rough life. I could tell from the sound of his voice that he had poured a lot of whisky over his vocal chords, and the creases on his face showed that he had been sad, he had been angry, and he had spent time squinting into the sunlight. He was dressed in cowboy boots, jeans, and a brown leather jacket. He was probably only in his mid-forties, but many of those forty or so years had been hard ones, and they had left their marks.

He had a pocketknife with a blade at least four inches long and throughout our conversation he played with it, flicking the blade out with a quick motion, and then closing it again. Flicking it out, and then closing it again. I was worried that he would accidentally close it on his fingers, and I watched him nervously while he flicked and closed, flicked and closed. I wasn't worried about myself. I didn't think that he would stab me, even though there was something wild and uneven in his eyes and in the shaky timbre of his voice. I kept seeing a vision of him catching his hand between the blade and the handle as he snapped it shut and chopping all those fingers off with one violent motion of the knife. It put me on edge.

He had turned the conversation in the direction of his writing and I sensed that he was only moments away from telling me about the book that those deadly cigarettes were helping him to write. I didn't have to wait long.

"I have a story. I need to tell it. It's a science fiction story."

I hadn't expected this. I had assumed I was in for either a western or a Hemingway rip-off.

"I like science fiction."

"It's based on a true story, about Joseph Haydn."

I wasn't sure how a novel could at once be based on a true story, be about Joseph Haydn, and also be science fiction. But I didn't interrupt.

"What do you know about Haydn?" He asked.

"Not much. He was a composer."

"He was an extraordinary man. He wrote 106 symphonies, when most composers can't be bothered to write more than nine. Some composers are frightened to write more than nine. They're a bunch of superstitious cowards. Beethoven, you see, only wrote nine and apparently those who attempt to outdo him come to bad ends. Haydn was smart enough to die before Beethoven, though, and he escaped the wrath of his unholy specter.

"He was an old man when he died on May 31, 1809. They held a funeral for him; there were lots of big shots there because he was a big shot himself. One of those big shots was Prince Nikolaus Esterhazy, one of the most aristocratic of the aristocrats in the old Austro-Hungarian Empire. He was buried in a humble grave, paid for by Esterhazy, but the prince planned to move him to a grander tomb when one could be built to accommodate his illustrious bones."

I noticed a few things as he related the plot to his novel. The first was that he never stopped flicking that knife open,

94

and then flicking it shut again. The second was that as he related his story, his way of speaking changed. He seemed to use bigger words suddenly. Writerly words. And his voice changed too. His tones were smoother, less conversational, more dramatic. It was like listening to an audiobook with a skilled reader narrating, but he wasn't reading any text, he was pulling his words directly from his brain as he spoke.

"A few nights after Haydn's funeral the stabbing noise of a shovel being repeatedly thrust into the earth could be heard ringing out over the quiet of the graveyard. The soft dirt, so recently piled on top of the composer, was being removed again. The gravedigger was shoveling his way down to the body he had just buried, like a sinner returning to his sin.

"Once he reached the coffin, he pulled it open. The body had been dead for four days and you can imagine the smell that greeted the gravedigger. But he was used to it. Death held no horrors for him. I wonder if what he did next horrified him though. I think even a tough old piece of leather like that gravedigger must have thought twice about what he did next. I'm no coward and I know that I would have. Because the next thing he did was saw Haydn's head off. I don't know what kind of saw he used, but you can bet it was no surgical instrument. It must have been a plain old wood saw, manufactured with carpentry in mind. It might have still had sawdust clinging to its edge. It might have been a little rusty. We can't know for sure 200 years after the fact, but what we do know is that this grave digger pulled that body out of the coffin, and, positioning it so that he could get at the neck, he placed the teeth of that saw against the bloodless skin, and he started to drag it back and forth.

"It must have been hard work, and if he hadn't become sweaty while digging up the body, he must have started to

95

sweat now that he was sawing at it. I can almost see those drops sliding down his forehead, collecting dirt as they went, sliding across his stubbly cheeks and jaws, and then dropping onto the fine silk suit that Haydn had been buried in.

"Once the head had been cut from the body, he shoved the now headless corpse back into the casket and slammed it shut again. I'm sure he would have liked to run away at this point. But he didn't. He put the head down on the tombstone and it watched him as he piled the dirt back into place.

"You're probably asking, 'Why would anyone do this?'

"Well, Haydn was considered the father of the symphony and string quartets. And unlike many classical composers, he was fortunate enough to figure out how to make money with his music. The artist is lucky who discovers the secret of turning art into money. He was one of the rare keepers of this sacred alchemical knowledge. Haydn's music was beautiful, so beautiful that it had attracted deep pocketed patrons like Prince Esterhazy. It's not just any music that can do that. It must be music of a magical kind.

"Haydn's life coincided with the invention of the science of phrenology. I'm using the term 'science' in the loosest sense here, because phrenology has, in fact, been thoroughly debunked and nowadays we laugh at its adherents and compare them to bloodletters and flat earthers. And we have a right to laugh at them, especially since their ideas were used to prop up racist ideologies through the time of the Civil War. But I think we should be careful, because if history has taught us anything, it is that future generations will hold our beliefs up to scorn someday too, no matter how certain we are in their solid certitude and bedrock rightness.

"Phrenology was the study of head bumps. If you run your fingers through your hair you will notice that your head has gentle undulations, ridges, ravines, and declivities. The Phrenologists believed that by interpreting a man's bumps you could learn a lot about him. Bumps, or the lack of them, could tell you if a man was a good man or a bad one, a law abider or a criminal, an intellectual or a blockhead, a courageous lion or a milquetoast pantywaist.

"Remember that a man's brain is hiding under a very thin crust of skull, and the brain is all. It is where not only your intelligence and your reason are housed; it is also the place that generates your feelings. Love isn't a product of the heart; it is the product of the brain. The brain is YOU, and with all that it's doing down there under that thin crust of skull people thought that surely it must shape the skull itself. As the convection currents of magma at the earth's mantle move the Earth's plates, throw up volcanos, and form mountain ridges, surely the power of the brain must exert a similar influence on the skull! This is not an argument that any of Haydn's contemporaries would have used, since plate tectonics hadn't been invented yet, but I think if they had known about plate tectonics they would have liked my comparison. If the part of the brain providing intelligence is strong, a bump will be in evidence on the portion of the skull above it, and the same goes for the parts that generate evil, lust, anger, and even artistic abilities.

"At the time of Haydn's death the believers in this science (for scientific theories have their believers and agnostics just as religious faiths do) were still trying to crack certain parts of the code presented by the human skull. While the first chemists were isolating elements, these pioneers of the mind were charting bumps and their meanings. Haydn's head would show the place in the brain where musical talent resided.

97

"I don't know how long that gravedigger sat in his house, alone with Haydn's head. I like to imagine him sitting at the table, with the head placed before him like a centerpiece, just staring at it while the head stared back, waiting for the sound of carriage wheels to signal the head's departure.

"When the carriage showed up there were two men inside. These men were Joseph Rosenbaum, Esterhazy's former secretary, and Johann Peter, Rosenbaum's friend. They were excited to get their hands on such a valuable scientific artifact, and they happily paid off the gravedigger for his services. I imagine their excitement was damped by the smell. They gagged and retched all the way home.

"After probing at the rotting head with their gentlemanly fingers, they found what they took for the bump of musical genius, and then sent the head off for the maceration of the flesh and bleaching of the skull. Rosenbaum was proud of his trophy. He had a beautiful black wooden box constructed to hold it. The box was decorated with a golden lyre to symbolize the connection of that head with music, and the skull sat on a white cushion inside. The box had glass windows so visitors could admire its contents.

"A decade later Esterhazy remembered his intention to give the great composer a more fitting tomb, and he had the casket dug up. You can't dig up a casket without peeking inside, and you can imagine everyone's surprise when the head wasn't in there along with the rest of Haydn. Esterhazy was no fool and he guessed at once who had done it. He sent men to search Rosenbaum's house, but Rosenbaum hid the skull in a mattress. His wife lay on the mattress and said they couldn't search the bed because she was having her period. They had a good old fashion fear of a woman's time of the month back then, and they didn't search.

98

"Eventually Rosenbaum gave a skull to Esterhazy and the Prince had it placed in the coffin and buried with the rest of Haydn in his new tomb. But the skull wasn't Haydn's. It was an imposter. The real skull rolled through history, being owned by a succession of strange men who had an interest in possessing such things, until 1954 when it came into the possession of somebody who though it right to give it back to its owner. Haydn's tomb was opened again and the skull was placed inside, right next to the imposter skull which was not removed, and then the tomb was closed back up."

I was quiet for a moment and waited for more as he lit another cigarette and blew out a massive cloud of smoke. I thought that he had only paused in his story so that he could light up again, but I was wrong. The story was over.

"I thought you said that you had written a science fiction story."

"I did. You see, the twist is that they are all robots. All of them. In my novel Haydn, Rosenbaum, the gravedigger, Peter, Esterhazy, all of them are robots." He threw his only partially smoked cigarette on the ground and walked off into the night.

Chapter 15

I slept in the bank entryway again. Rain fell all night, but the bank kept me dry. When I awoke, I saw two pigeons picking at a chicken bone just inches from my head. I hadn't eaten since lunch the day before and was so hungry that I almost fought them for it.

After rousing myself from my cardboard bed I went directly to a dingy bakery where I bought a cup of coffee and a couple doughnuts with the previous day's panhandling proceeds. I kept my sips and my bites small as I lingered over someone else's discarded morning paper. The slower I ate, the longer I could sit in the warm bakery. The baker glared at me and the rest of the business's patrons kept as far away as possible in our small shared space. I did not smell good. I was the natural man, a piece of meat stewed in its own juices, and you could almost see an odoriferous haze surrounding my body like a demonic aura.

Okay, now, I'm going to talk about excrement for a bit, so, if you have a tender stomach or standards of some kind you may want to skim or skip the next few pages. I don't want to talk about it, but, well, things have happened that make it necessary. To leave the subject out of this narrative would feel like an evasion.

I was wandering around Pacific Heights, admiring the homes of my former neighbors, when the urge to poop hit me. The moment I felt the first stirrings I knew that I was in trouble. The pressure immediately built, and the situation became critical within seconds. There were only homes around me, and I couldn't very well knock on someone's door and ask to use their bathroom. It would be very embarrassing for one thing, and for another, who in their right mind would let me in? If a greasy street person arrived on your doorstep and begged you wildly to let him use your toilet, would you do it? Would you let a dirty, agitated, and possibly insane vagrant into your house to use that most intimate of appliances? I did not dare to gamble on the goodwill of my fellow man.

Instead, I hurried down Pacific, pausing at frequent intervals to cross my legs and clench my buttocks. I had at least five blocks to go until I hit Van Ness, a commercial street where I would be able to find some businesses that might allow me to use their toilet. As I walked, I began to feel a searing pain in my guts. It was as if I had eaten something hard and sharp but also alive and very angry. The pain became more intense by the second and I could feel my face alternately flushing red and draining white with the stabs of agony.

I began to sweat. A monster was trying to gnaw its way out of the maze of my innards, and the pain and terrible effort of keeping it inside my body drove me to perspire. Hideous odors that had been waiting in their subcutaneous realms now sprang forth with the effusion of new perspiration. The cocktail of old and new sweat was suffocating in its repulsiveness and I knew that the stench would make convincing some shopkeeper to allow me to use his bathroom even more difficult. With only one block to go the unholy child was threatening to crown at any moment, but I could not run, doing so would have permitted the turd to slip the surly bonds of my colon and touch the face of my pants.

Finally, I arrived at a convenience store. I clenched my cheeks and waddled miserably to the clerk who was ensconced behind the protective force field of his expansive desk.

"Can I use your bathroom?"

He did not answer immediately. He looked me over slowly with all the aloofness of an Olympian deity. He was a black bearded Arab and when he finally spoke his voice was colored with an accent that I would have found charming under different circumstances. "Bathroom, for customer only."

"But I really have to go!" Sweat was dripping down my forehead and gathering in the bog of my eyebrows. I shifted my weight uneasily from foot to foot and my frame was slightly bent at the waist in a poor attempt to accommodate the unwieldy load I carried within me.

"You buy gas?"

"No."

"You buy candy bar?"

"No."

"You buy alcohol?"

"No."

"You buy Forbes magazine?"

"No."

"Then no bathroom."

"Fine," the pressure was killing me, "I'll take a Butterfinger. Now give me the key to the bathroom please!" I could see the key on the wall behind the man's desk. It was a slim piece of copper attached to a crushed beer can by a chain.

"No, Butterfinger not enough, alcohol too. Five dollar, must spend five dollar."

My face was already quite scarlet by this point, otherwise it would have reddened now with anger. There I stood, a man who was clearly suffering unspeakable agony, and this other man, sitting in his comfortable swivel chair, watching the Game Show Network and eating a Slim Jim, had decided to take advantage of me. I was outraged. There are profits to be made in immediate suffering (hospital emergency rooms operate on this same principle) and this man was determined to make them.

A combination of physical agony and mental rage closed around me and I felt myself swoon. A thousand violent fantasies flashed through my brain in the space of a few seconds. In each of them the man before me was subjected to unspeakable torture. I could not bow to this man. I could not! I fled shrieking obscenities. The man behind the desk had no reaction to my departure other than to warm up his Slim Jim with a cigarette lighter and to redirect his glance towards his small television set.

Once back outside I looked about me wildly for another toilet. There was a deli right next to the gas station and I minced into it on tiptoe. It was vacant except for a teenager behind the counter.

"Can I use your bathroom?" I asked with the voice of a more-pathetic-than-average Dickensian orphan.

"You gonna buy a sandwich?"

I went black inside at the suggestion. "No, I just need to use the toilet. . . please?"

He looked at me a moment as if trying to decide whether my agony was sincere. Finally, he mumbled, "Ah, what do I care? My shift is almost over and I ain't gonna clean it." And then he handed me a key. Once inside I let the door close behind me as I fumbled at my pants buttons with shaking fingers. It was all over before my bottom even hit the cold plastic of the toilet seat. An intense feeling of relief flooded over my entire frame. This is how Sisyphus would undoubtedly feel if he ever put his boulder on the top of the hill, or Tantalus would feel if he was ever allowed to take that drink. I sat there for a moment, trembling in silent joy. The battle was won, the trousers remained clean. When I stood, I turned for a moment to gaze at the vanquished foe.

It sat there, only partially submerged, like the hulk of some great ship that has foundered in shallow water.

Not having a home complicates everything. Home is where your heart is, but also where your bathroom is.

Chapter 16

My Grandfather was a marine and he served in the Pacific Theater during the Second World War. He had a bullet nick his ear at Tarawa and a piece of shrapnel take a chunk of his arm at Iwo Jima, but he always maintained that the worst injury he sustained during the war was a severe case of athlete's foot. Good pedal hygiene is not always possible when you're fighting for your life in some sweltering jungle nightmare. When you spend every waking moment (and in those conditions almost all your moments are waking moments) just trying to avoid dying, you tend to forget things like properly bathing your feet and changing your socks at regular intervals. So a fungus, which existed only the stinking, soggy, corpse-strewn battlefields of the Pacific, took root between his neglected toes.

It began with a little tickle between the big toe on his right foot and the smaller toe next to it. The tickle soon spread to the rest of his toes on both feet. Next, the tickle intensified to an itch. Then the itch became one of the trials of Job. It plagued him night and day. At every chance he would tear his boots from his feet and scratch his toes with dirty fingernails. The skin on his feet began to die, exposing a raw pink layer beneath. Then blood began to ooze from the sores. His itchy toes were now inflamed with pain and they sloshed around all day in a mixture of blood, sweat, jungle muck, and fungal discharge. And despite the intensity of the pain, the itching continued, as ferocious as ever.

Grandpa was not a complainer. His suffering grew so overwhelming, however, that he was reduced to walking on his heels and was eventually forced to see a doctor. The doctor, who seemed unaware of the exigencies of jungle warfare, ordered him to keep his feet clean and dry and to change his socks three times per day. Grandpa was also given a bottle of powdered fungicide and was told to sprinkle the poison over his toes after every washing.

I only bring this up because I now know what it must have been like for him. Two days ago, I felt the first little tickle between my toes. In the intervening time this tickle has intensified to a raging itch and I am afraid that pain and bleeding are the next step. My feet have been stuck inside the same pair of soiled Haynes brand tube socks ever since I stepped out of my apartment. They are positively slimy. They have become fungus incubators.

I have been out on the street begging for the past couple of days, but I have been able to take in only a little more money than I need to spend on food. Right now I have seven dollars in my pocket. I went to price athlete's foot remedies a moment ago and have discovered that there are none to be had for under thirteen dollars at the nearest Walgreens. This is a problem. In addition to medication I am going to need to buy a new pair of socks so that I can have something to wear while I wash these ones out. I will not be able to eat today if I want to fix my feet, and I would much rather go hungry than face any more of this incessant itching that no amount of frenzied scratching seems to assuage.

Chapter 17

Motivated by my itching feet and determined to succeed as a panhandler, I took in over thirty dollars of revenue in just a few hours. I constructed a sign that said, "Please help, I am in agony!" but was not content to let the written word alone speak for me. I volubly accosted those who passed me by. "Come on, I need a dollar! Please? How about a quarter then?" I made eye-contact with every man who dared to turn his face in my direction. When they looked at me, they instantly read the script of pain scratched upon my face. Finding me worthy of their largess they parted with their dimes and nickels, with their quarters and fifty cent pieces, and even with their crisp newly minted one dollar bills. The moment I had enough money for socks and antifungal foot powder I ran to Walgreens on my heels while yelping "ouch, ouch, ouch," with every step. I made my purchases and then bathed my feet in a park drinking fountain to the obvious dismay of all witnesses. They were discomfited by the sight of a bum putting his feet where they sometimes put their faces. Once my feet were clean, I allowed them to air dry in the cool bay breezes.

Air and sunshine are powerful medicine.

I lay in the grass for a good twenty minutes, enjoying the soothing sensation of fresh air running through the gaps between my tortured toes. Once my feet were dry, I dusted them heavily with antifungal foot powder. The powder on my feet resembled confectioner's sugar on a pastry. I was hungry. Ignoring my hunger, I reclined on the lawn and fell asleep. The unbearable agony of raging athlete's foot had prevented all but the most fleeting scraps of sleep the night before. I was awakened by the roar of a passing bus about a half hour after nodding off, but I had rested enough to feel

107

invigorated. I pulled my new socks over my red toes and inserted my feet into my boots. I then washed my filthy, stinking, sticky old socks in the drinking fountain and hung them from straps on the back of my pack so that they could dry out.

Though my feet were still itchy and sore, I felt much better. I found bitter satisfaction in the thought that the fungus that had caused me so much suffering in the past couple of days was being poisoned to death. I hoped fungus was capable of feeling pain and that it was conscious of the meaning of death, although I had my doubts on both counts. I returned to my corner on Van Ness and Sutter and began to beg once again. I no longer carried the air of the suffering mendicant however; I now approached the job with the vim and vigor of a carnival freak show hustler. I had a smile for all who passed before me. I wished the world well, and the world responded. Nickels, dimes, quarters and dollars poured into my bursting coffers, and when the day was done, I had twenty seven dollars to my name. I spent six of them on the finest meal to be had at Kentucky Fried Chicken and blew another two on a paperback I fished out of the bargain bin at a used bookstore.

With a successful day behind me I limped back to my home at the bank. I sat on the stack of cardboard I had inherited from Rick and began to read my book in the soft glow of the streetlights. My feet were still hurting and itching, but I was clearly on the road to recovery. I took off my boots to air out my toes and I applied another layer of powder. Life was good.

Americans love the earnest go-getter in all aspects of society. Our favorite billionaires are of the "self-made" variety, and we despise those who are born to money. The most beloved members of the local sports team are not the ones who have the most athletic gifts, they are the ones who "hustle," and play "for the love of the game." Even among beggars we prefer the one who hustles to the meek soul who submissively sits on the corner, saying nothing as he raises one dirty hand with the palm facing upward in silent supplication. We may resent the brash tactics of the man who yells at us "GIVE ME A DOLLAR!" but we admire his can-do spirit. On the other hand, the man who sits on the pavement with a doleful look smeared across his pock-marked face while quietly mumbling something about his terrible hunger earns nothing but our contempt. We want to tell him to get a job, while in some sense we feel that the aggressive panhandler already *has* a job.

I'd become one of those aggressive panhandlers. Necessity had stripped my pride away and I no longer felt shame in baldly asking people for handouts. I could finally panhandle with the proper attitude. Gone was the bowed headed mendicant of the day before! I was a new man, and I could see no reason why I couldn't pull in forty dollars a day if I really made an effort.

A storm brewed up in the late afternoon and a hard wind drove raindrops into pedestrians like machine gun bullets. The rain caught me in the open while wandering down Market Street and I was soaked while I scrambled across the puddled pavement in search of shelter. I found a deeply recessed doorway bracketed by big glass display windows that had been pasted over with newspapers and I leaped into it as if bombs had begun to fall around me and it was a concrete bunker.

One of the many terrible things about living on the street is the fact that when you get wet, there is no way to dry out again. You have to stew in your own cold juices, the prunes on the tips of your fingers refusing to smooth back out. As I sat in my doorway, out of the rain but wet and miserable, I remembered my high school science teacher explaining why being wet makes us cold. Mr. Siufanua, a large man of Polynesian descent who doubled as the school's football coach, had explained that when a liquid turns into a gas (as when water evaporates from the skin), it needs energy, and it takes that energy from its surroundings. The energy it sucks up is usually in the form of heat, and this heat leaves with the evaporating liquid, making the surroundings cooler.

But knowing why I was cold didn't make me any warmer.

I wanted to get into my sleeping bag, but if I got into it with my wet clothes, I'd have a wet sleeping bag. The obvious thing to do was to strip naked and only then climb into it, but Market Street is a busy place and I still had enough pride to not want to be seen naked in public, plus I had to assume that even in San Francisco the sight of a naked homeless man might make one of the locals call the police. I balled myself up, wrapped my arms around my knees, and shivered. I was miserable.

It wouldn't have been so bad without the wind. It was a merciless, evil, chilling wind. A killing wind that in the old days would have driven ships onto the rocks around the Golden Gate. It was an umbrella destroying wind. A face slapping wind. Sometimes it would seem to subside for a few seconds, but then would come back hard and hit me like a snowball to the neck.

During my time living on the street I hadn't once spent a night in a homeless shelter. Part of me knew that if I was sincere about studying the plight of the homeless I should probably do that, but another part of me felt that because I was on the streets by choice I shouldn't take the bed of another person who was actually in need. But then another part of me said that this was just a cop out, and that the real reason I didn't want to sleep in a shelter was that I was worried it would be packed with diseased people who smelled bad and who might also possibly stab me in my sleep. The debate had been going on in my brain for several days now in this circular fashion, but I was so miserable at this moment that I knew I had to either find a shelter, or just give up on the whole project, go home, take a hot shower, and fall asleep in my own warm bed.

Just as my discomfort and despair were reaching climax, a gust of wind, more powerful than any of the gusts that had preceded it, pushed into that doorway with so much force that the door behind me made a loud creaking noise and then actually swung open. I regarded this as a sign and quickly scampered in, shutting it behind me.

It was the middle of the day, but the sunlight was being filtered through a thick bed of black clouds, and then through the newspapers taped to the building's windows, leaving only a milky darkness inside. My eyes adjusted slowly, the room gradually taking shape as I stood there and listened to the hypnotic sound of the rain falling just outside. I could also hear wind whistling through the building, but from where I stood all was still, not a breath of it brushed against my skin.

The room I was standing in had once been a retail space, maybe a shoe or clothing store, but now it was stripped bare, right down to the concrete floors. I took a few steps deeper into the building, my footfalls sounding loud in the big, empty, quiet space. There wasn't anything about the place to inspect or explore, except for a door on the far side. I walked away from the soft glow coming from the newspapered windows where I had come in and moved towards that door on the darker side of the room.

I don't know why, but I hesitated before turning the doorknob. I was, for reasons I couldn't quite explain, a bit

111

scared to open it. But I didn't have anything else do to, so I turned the knob.

I was surprised to see light in the next room. It was candlelight, and my first thought was, "SATANIC RITUAL! SATANIC RITUAL! I HAVE STUMBLED ONTO A SATANIC RITUAL!" But this irrational jolt of fear subsided when I realized that there was only one person in that back room, and that she was an old woman. She looked very much like a witch, with her wild hair and hooked nose, but my rational brain had reasserted itself over my lizard brain, and my voice sounded calm when I said, "Oh, I'm sorry, I didn't realize that anybody was in here."

The room was very dark. A small amount of light dribbled in from the door I had just opened, but there were no windows, and the only other light was from the three candles the woman had placed on the floor around her. She didn't seem scared or upset by my appearance, and she asked, "Are you the owner of the building?"

"No. Just homeless right now, and looking for a place to crash."

"Well you can crash in here if you like."

"Thanks. I'll settle into this other room, if that's okay."

"Stay for a while. I haven't left this building in three days, and I've been hoping someone would find their way in here to talk to me."

I didn't want to stay. The woman seemed deranged as she sat in her pile of dirty blankets surrounded by her feeble candles. They were the short, stubby, unscented kind of candle that one might use on Halloween to illuminate a jack-o-lantern. But how could I say "no" to this lonely old woman sitting by herself in the candlelight? I'm pretty selfish, but every once in a while you have to knuckle under to your conscience and do the decent thing. So, I sat on a wooden chair with its backrest broken off, the only piece of furniture in the room, and settled in for a chat.

"What's your novel about?" She asked.

It was with a sense of relief that I realized I had an answer of sorts to this question now. "Well, I… I haven't started writing it yet, not really, but it's about a guy with a bland life and a boring job and no girlfriend and no ideas for a novel."

"I say this in a spirit of constructive criticism, but that sounds boring. Really boring."

"Yes. I suppose it does."

"What happens to your protagonist?"

"He falls in love."

"That's been done."

"I know."

"Many, many times."

"I know that. He knows that. One of the reasons he doesn't want to become a novelist is that he is terribly aware of the fact that everything has been done, many, many times."

"Okay, so, he falls in love. Then what?"

"It shakes him. He realizes that his life has been bland and colorless. And she, the woman he falls in love with, she represents flavor, and color. She represents emotion, and heart, and soul."

"Sounds trite."

"I know. I know it does."

"Does she like him?"

"He hopes so."

"Ha! He should know it! If they don't let you know it the answer is probably no, they don't love you. I've learned this to my cost. What does he do to win her over?"

"He, uh, he, uh, he, um, decides to write a novel?"

"About her?"

"After he meets her, everything he says and does is in some way or another about her."

She laughed at that, "Hopeless. Terrible and corny. Predictable. And I can't give you any constructive criticism anyway when your book is clearly about you! It's basically a memoir, isn't it?"

"Maybe. I haven't written it yet, so it's hard to say what it might be. I'm researching it."

"Ah" she said, as if I'd just explained something she had been wondering about, "So, am I going to be a character in your book?"

"Almost certainly."

"Make sure to mention that I look like a witch. I do look like a witch; don't you think? With this nose and this hair?"

It seemed impolite to agree with her on this point, so I changed the subject. "What's your book about?"

"Read it." She was sitting next to a stack of papers, and she pushed them towards me now.

It was a thick stack. There had to be at least 2,000 sheets of paper in it, and my instinct was to recoil in horror from such a manuscript. Two thousand pages from an unpublished crazy lady who was squatting in the back room of an abandoned store? They couldn't be good. There was no chance they were good. Did she expect me to sit there and read these 2,000 pages in front of her, while she watched like a grandmother hoping to see her grandchildren enjoy the tuna casserole she has made for Sunday dinner? It is true that I was bored, but not doing anything at all is a passive and almost enjoyable sort of boredom, whereas the boredom of reading a bad book is a hateful variety.

"You don't have to read all of it. Just give that first page a try. I think you'll like it."

I was skeptical, but a page couldn't hurt. That first page was a piece of white, unlined paper, and the words on it were written in small but neat handwriting, in black ink.

London. Michaelmas term lately over, and the Lord Chancellor sitting in Lincoln's Inn Hall. Implacable November weather. As much mud in the streets as if the waters had but newly retired from the face of the earth, and it would not be wonderful to meet a Megalosaurus, forty feet long or so, waddling like an elephantine lizard up Holborn Hill. Smoke lowering down from chimney-pots, making a soft black drizzle, with flakes of soot in it as big as full-grown snowflakes—gone into mourning, one might imagine, for the death of the sun. Dogs, undistinguishable in mire. Horses, scarcely better; splashed to their very blinkers. Foot passengers, jostling one another's umbrellas in a general infection of ill temper, and losing their foot-hold at street-corners, where tens of thousands of other foot passengers have been slipping and sliding since the day broke (if this day ever broke), adding new deposits to the crust upon crust of mud, sticking at those points tenaciously to the pavement, and accumulating at compound interest.

It was, I had to admit to myself, a magnificent opening paragraph. It also sounded very familiar. "Is this Dickens?"

"It's mine now. It was his, but he's dead and it's mine now. I call it *Bleak House*. I've also written books called *Hard Times*, *Nicholas Nickleby*, and *Oliver Twist*."

"But," and then I paused, because it's a bad idea to argue with a crazy person, especially when you are hoping to share their shelter for the night. "But Charles Dickens wrote all of those books."

"They are all mine now."

"Have you published them?"

"I have submitted them to a number of agents and publishers, only to be rejected. It never pays to cast your pearls before swine. But I have self-published them. You can buy them on Amazon. Just look up '*Bleak House*, by Sandra Blickenstaff' and you'll see."

"Do people buy these books?"

"They are on sale on Amazon. You can get the longer ones for $20 and *Hard Times* for just $10."

"But does anyone buy them?"

"NO! Because Dickens is somehow still selling his books from beyond the grave, and you can get them for free on the internet. It's not fair! It's anticompetitive! He's been rich and famous for 150 years while I squat in any broken down building I can find even though I've written a masterpiece like *Bleak House*! People go to Dickens festivals where they all gather around, watching stage productions of *A Christmas Carol* and listening to seminars about how great Boz is while I sit here on my pile of rags in the candlelight! It's not fair! Not fair!"

"Well," I put forth timidly, "he did write them first."

She just glared at me. I thought it best to soothe her. "That's a great first paragraph."

"Isn't it?" she said warmly, instantly brightening and not noticing that I hadn't attributed the paragraph to her. "So evocative. A brutal picture of London in the rain during Victorian times. Savagely beautiful. I'm very proud of it. What's your first line?"

"I was thinking something like, 'Whether I shall turn out to be the hero of my own life, or whether that station will be held by anybody else, these pages must show.'"

Her eyes narrowed and her brow boiled up into a terrible set of furrows. For a moment I thought she might make an objection, but instead she let her face go smooth again (at least, as smooth as it was capable of getting) and she said, "That's very good."

"I thought you would appreciate it."

"And have you ever been published?"

"No."

"But you're going to try to get this love story of yours published?"

"I don't know."

She cackled at my response and said, "Oh sure. Everyone is writing for an audience. Of course you want to be published. You're writing for them!" She gestured to a huge multitude of imaginary people who inhabited all the room's dark corners.

"I'm just writing for the girl, really. She's dating this awful guy who has published a volume of short stories called *Vulcan's Vestigial Third Nipple*, I'm going to one up him with my novel. Assuming I get published. Which seems unlikely."

"Don't lose heart, young man," she said, "remember that *Carrie*, by Stephen King, was rejected thirty times before it went on to make him rich and famous." I knew it. In this world where everyone is writing a novel, everyone knows that *Carrie* was rejected 30 times. This is the consolation that aspiring writers repeat to themselves as a mantra whenever a Self-Addressed Stamped Envelope full of rejection lands in their mailbox. Thirty times. I knew that she was about the repeat the rest of the sacred litany. "*A Wrinkle in Time* was rejected twenty-six times. *Dune* was rejected twenty-three times. And even *The Diary of Anne Frank* was rejected fifteen times. After all she suffered, to get 15 rejections before her bestselling critical triumph! Harry Potter himself," she seemed to think that Harry Potter was an actual person who wrote the Harry Potter books, "was rejected no fewer than twelve times. TWELVE!" She

117

said this in triumph, as if this fact conclusively demonstrated that all her rejections were proof of her excellence. "And listen to this… I have it here somewhere… it's a rejection letter for *Moby Dick*… AH! Here it is!"

After rifling through a pile of dirty papers behind her she came out with a scrap and read it with a voice of mock pomposity, "First, we must ask, does it have to be a whale? While this is a rather delightful, if somewhat esoteric, plot device, we recommend an antagonist with a more popular visage among the younger readers. For instance, could not the Captain be struggling with a depravity towards young, perhaps voluptuous, maidens?" She crackled with laughter, "Can you imagine writing such a ridiculous letter to Herman Melville! I may write *Moby Dick* someday myself, and when I do, I hope I get exactly this letter of rejection. I would feed on my scorn for a month."

She didn't say anything for a while and as I studied her face I could tell that she was imagining what it would be like to get such a letter in response to her submission of *Moby Dick* to Little, Brown and Company.

"Well, I hate to leave you alone, but do you mind if I go back to the other room so I can crawl into my sleeping bag and get some rest. I'm freezing."

"Go ahead. Would you like to take my book with you to read?"

I started to reject her offer, but then I remembered that her book was *Bleak House*. "Yes, I'd enjoy that very much." Her eyes glowed with pride as I gathered up the pages and disappeared into the next room. I peeled back the newspaper on the display window just enough to get some light, pulled off my wet clothes and set them out to dry, scratched and powdered my toes, and then crawled into my warm sleeping bag and began to read.

Fog everywhere. Fog up the river, where it flows among green aits and meadows; fog down the river, where it rolls defiled among the tiers of shipping and the waterside pollutions of a great (and dirty) city. Fog on the Essex marshes, fog on the Kentish heights. Fog creeping into the cabooses of collier-brigs; fog lying out on the yards and hovering in the rigging of great ships; fog drooping on the gunwales of barges and small boats. Fog in the eyes and throats of ancient Greenwich pensioners, wheezing by the firesides of their wards; fog in the stem and bowl of the afternoon pipe of the wrathful skipper, down in his close cabin; fog cruelly pinching the toes and fingers of his shivering little 'prentice boy on deck. Chance people on the bridges peeping over the parapets into a nether sky of fog, with fog all round them, as if they were up in a balloon and hanging in the misty clouds."

It fit my mood perfectly. I liked Sandra's second paragraph almost as much as her first.

I read for three hours, tucked in my sleeping bag with my back resting against the window and the manuscript held up to the weak sunlight. When night fell a light from across the street kept me turning pages for a couple hours more, until warm and dry and sated with reading I slumped over and fell asleep on the concrete floor.

Chapter 18

The realization that I wasn't really experiencing life as a homeless person crept up on me day by day. I didn't have the same miserable past that real street people did, nor did I have any sense of what it was like to have a hopeless future. I came from a warm, safe, and loving past, and after a few weeks on the street I was going to plug myself right back into my bright future. The only way I was going to get a real feel for what it was like to live on the streets for days and years on end would be if I talked to legitimately homeless people. I would have to get my experience second hand.

As I wandered up Market Street the morning after I met the author of *Bleak House,* I saw two people perched on the concrete slabs of the UN Plaza Fountain who looked like good candidates for interviews. I watched surreptitiously from about thirty feet away for about ten minutes before I approached them. One of the two was a black man with matted dreadlocks, probably in his mid-thirties, who was wearing a filthy mechanic's jumpsuit and occasionally drinking from a bottle hidden in a brown paper bag. He was talking to a white woman, about his same age. She was dressed in baggy acid washed jeans and a pink sweater with a black vest. She also had dreadlocks and was also drinking something that she hid in a brown paper bag. Each of them had a shopping cart parked next to the concrete slab. Despite all their drinking I got a sense that they were more or less coherent and would be able to talk about things.

The fountain was struggling that day. It hadn't been switched off, but somehow there didn't seem to be enough water pressure to shoot jets and streams into the air. The fountain spattered gushes of green liquid in ragged spasms from time to time, like the dying gasps of a beached whale. I strolled up to the couple and climbed on to their slab.

"You guys mind if I join you?" I asked.

"Naw, man, do whatever you want to do," the man said.

"Thanks," I replied. Once I was on top of the slab and sitting cross legged, we were all awkwardly quiet for a moment before I observed, "Chilly today. Misty even."

"Yeah," the woman responded.

"This'll take the nip off," I said as I hoisted a bottle of Colt 45 out of my backpack. I opened it up and as I did the sour aroma of the bottle's contents tweaked my nose. I had brought the bottle to give some authenticity to my pose as a bum, but now that I was confronted with the prospect of actually drinking it, I quailed. I took a nip. It was so gross. I should have gone with cheap vodka instead. "Either of you guys want to take a pull?" I offered, hopping one or the other of them would greedily drink it all so I wouldn't have to. To my surprise, they both declined.

"What a life," I said, hoping it would somehow spark them into conversation.

"Yeah." they said in unison.

And then it was quiet for another few minutes.

I realized I was going to have to push them a bit to get their life stories. I took another pull at the Colt 45 and then asked, "Did you guys think your lives would ever come to this?"

Neither of them responded, although I sensed that each hoped that the other would respond. Hoping didn't make it happen. I was going to have to be even more direct.

"How did you end up on the streets?" I asked the man.

He didn't answer right away, and when he did his words were somehow bumbling and unsure. "Ah, you know how it is. Grew up rough. Dad in jail. Single mama raisin' a bunch of us kids on welfare. Beatin' us every night for supper. I

121

started runnin' with a rough crowd, drinkin' too much of this," he held his bagged bottle up for inspection, "lookin' for happiness in the bottom of a bottle. And now I'm here."

I had listened attentively, and I noticed that the woman had also listened carefully. But there wasn't much in the story. It sounded cliched, but I supposed that some things become cliché because they are common.

I turned to the woman, "How did you wind up living on the streets?"

She hesitated, and then began, "I had religious parents. They would beat us whenever we got out of line. My dad was an alcoholic. I ran away when I was 14, got pregnant, had the baby, and my parents put it up for adoption. I ran away again, got hooked on crack, got hooked on heroin, got hooked on meth, and started spending my nights out on the street. I've been in and out of jail so many times I can't even count it, all for little things like shoplifting, but it's hard to get a job when you have a record, and even harder when you have a habit. So I'm out here begging for a living, waiting to get stabbed in some back alley one night. Maybe my parents will care then."

Again. Cliché. I started to wonder if my plan to interview street people would be at all helpful. Then the woman asked me, "How about you? How did you end up on the streets?"

Uh oh. I hadn't ever thought to concoct a backstory, so I tried to construct one now on the fly. "Uh, well, uh, I had a rough childhood. My dad was in jail most of the time and my momma had to raise all us kids on welfare," I paused as I realized I was just regurgitating the story the man had told two minutes earlier. I decided it was hopeless and I'd better come clean, "I'm sorry, you guys, I'm not homeless. I'm just out here doing research for a book."

The woman seemed to slump in disappointment. "I'm researching a book too," she lifted the bottle out of her bag to show that she had been drinking kombucha.

Then the man said, "Neither of you is homeless? Why am I wasting my time with you guys? I would like to be able to research my novel without running into a bunch of white people playing pretend!" He stormed off in a huff, pushing his shopping cart towards the Civic Center. The woman also stormed off, pushing her cart in the opposite direction down Market Street. I sat alone by the fountain for a few minutes more, watching it gasp and sputter like a patient in the last stages of tuberculosis. As I watched the murky water spatter itself meaninglessly against the slabs, I suddenly remembered reading a story in the newspaper a few weeks earlier about how the homeless used the fountain as a toilet. Then I too hurried away.

Chapter 19

I slept in the narrow doorway of a closed restaurant that was just wide enough for me to lie down in. It was a nice spot, better sheltered from the wind than the bank had been, and I had my best night of sleep yet. There was a strong scent of stale urine in the air, but I was tired enough not to care. In the morning, however, at around seven, I was awakened by a gentle prodding in my ribs. My eyes opened to see a muscular fifty-year-old Latino with obsidian black hair and a steel gray handlebar moustache. He was poking me with a wooden yardstick.

"Excuse me," he said in a polite tone, "you can't sleep here."

"What do you care?" I asked with no small amount of irritation. I had been dreaming of Abby, and she vanished, along with almost all memory of the dream, as soon as the yardstick prodded me. Being awakened to my real life was disagreeable.

"I own this restaurant."

"Oh," I said.

"So, you've got to go."

I quickly sat up and wadded my sleeping bag into my backpack. Homeless though I was, I still had respect for private property, at least when the owner of the property was confronting me. "I'm sorry. I thought this place was closed."

"It is closed. I just bought it. I'm going to remodel the sucker and open it back up."

"Good luck."

The man studied me for a moment. "Would you be interested in working a few hours on the remodeling?"

"Uh . . . I really don't know anything about that sort of thing."

"You won't need to know anything. At this point it's just tearing out the old stuff before we put in new stuff. You interested?"

"How much are you paying me?"

"I'll give you four dollars an hour."

I thought about it. Would I be betraying my mission? The homeless took odd jobs from time to time, didn't they?

"How about five dollars an hour?"

"Four fifty."

"Done."

He pulled a wallet from his pocket and removed a five-dollar bill. He held it in his hand a long second, reconsidering the impulse that had brought the bill out of the warmth and security of his leather billfold and into the cold and foul smelling air.

"If I give this to you as an advance so you can get yourself some breakfast before you start working, are you going to just take it and run away?"

"Nope."

"You sure? I'd like you to eat because I think you'll work better on a full stomach."

"Yep."

"But I'd hate for you to take this five and just run off with easy money."

"It's a gamble; I'll grant you that."

"I'd ask you for some collateral, but I don't know what I could possibly do with any of your stuff if you left me holding the bag."

"You'd probably have to turn it over to the hazmat team."

He handed me the bill. "I've got to figure out a plan of attack here. Be back in a half hour and we'll start tearing the joint apart."

After eating a plate of greasy eggs and hurriedly slurping down hot mug of coffee I limped back to the restaurant.

"You came back," he seemed happily surprised.

"Yep."

"What's your name?"

"Daniel."

"I'm Antonio Sandoval, just call me Tony. Now grab a crowbar and let's start ripping things up."

We worked hard all morning. We pried up old benches that were bolted to the floor and broke them into smaller pieces so they would be easier to cart to the dump. We pulled up tables, tore the legs from them, split the tops in two, and tossed them onto the rubbish pile. We spent the morning listening to Tony's oldies station and sports talk radio. At lunchtime Tony gave me fifteen bucks and sent me to a nearby greasy spoon to pick up burgers and fries. He looked me over while we ate and finally asked a question. "So why is it that a guy like you is living on the street? You work ok, you don't look like a junkie; I don't get it. What's your story?"

I had taken a liking to Tony. Since I had hit the streets he was the first person to show some kind of compassionate interest in me, the first person to give me the benefit of the doubt, the first person who gave me a chance instead of a few coins. I didn't want to lie to him. I liked and respected him too much. At the same time, I didn't want to tell him the truth (whatever that was). The integrity of the project demanded that I be the only person who knew about it.

"I'm sorry Tony, but I'd rather not get into it."

"All right, I'm sorry I asked."

We went back to work. Between the prying, the hammering, the ripping, and the noise from the radio, Tony talked about himself. He had worked in construction most of

126

his life, but he had long dreamed of owning a restaurant. By providing labor at a third world price I was helping the man's dream to come true.

He told me about his book. He had already written 800 pages of what was to be the epic story of an illegal immigrant from Mexico who moves to the United States and becomes a rich and powerful real estate developer, only to have his past connections with the drug cartels come back to haunt him. To be honest, it sounded pretty good except for the part where it was already 800 pages long and seemed likely to go on for another 800 more. I asked Tony if he had considered slicing it up into a series, but he refused to even think about it. All 1,600 pages together would constitute a single work of art, he said, and nothing would compel him to dismember it. He reminded me of the story from the bible about the two women who both claimed to be mother of a baby. He said that he was his novel's true mother, and he would never consent to chopping it in half.

At about six he decided to call it a day. He turned to me and asked, "What did we agree on? Four dollars and fifty cents an hour I think?"

"Yep."

"I can't pay you that amount."

My blood ran cold. This man I had taken an instant liking to, this man whose company and confidences I had shared all day long, this man who I had assumed was charity personified, THIS MAN was going to rip me off! Me! I was a defenseless homeless man! I began mentally sketching out plans for retaliation. A brick through the window on opening night perhaps . . . but then I decided to tackle the issue head on.

"Why not," I asked, attempting to hide the slight tremble in my voice.

"Well, I thought you were a bum, so I proposed to pay you bum wages. I didn't think you'd be much of a worker, but you worked like a man, so I'll pay you a man's wage. How does that sound?"

I was dumbfounded. "Wait, so . . . you're renegotiating the deal upward?"

"Yes."

"Okay."

"I'll give you seventy dollars for the whole day, that's ten dollars per hour and subtracting the ten dollars for your lunch and breakfast."

I said "thank you" as he handed me three twenty-dollar bills and one ten dollar bill.

"Find yourself someplace to stay, and come back tomorrow, will you?"

I stepped out of the warm restaurant where we had been working and into the cool evening. I had what seemed an immense amount of money in my pocket and the promise of more the next day. With so much cash in hand I dashed into a secondhand clothing store and went on a mad spending spree. I bought a pair of pants and a shirt. I then went to a new clothing store and bought another pair of socks and a three pack of underwear.

The package of underwear was the most important item I purchased. Most people in the civilized world never go a day without changing their underwear. I had gone a week and a half. And it had not been a leisurely week and a half either. I had spent it walking, toiling, suffering, and sweating, and my underpants had paid the price. They were the underpants of the damned. They had turned a sweaty yellow and were emitting a noxious effluvium capable of euthanizing a mid-sized goat.

128

What was bothering me the most about my underwear was the fact that they had become intensely uncomfortable. The constant process of sweating and drying out had deposited large amounts of minerals in the fabric, and this had the effect of stiffening the cloth. My hardened underpants rubbed and chafed against my sensitive regions with every step. In the past couple of days, the flesh there had become raw and I had increasingly been forced to walk with a bow legged gait to minimize contact between the opposing soft and rough surfaces. My new underpants would be like a pillow between my thighs.

After I bought the clothes I needed I found a hotel in the Tenderloin where I could get a bed at a low, low price.

Chapter 20

Before beginning this experiment in homelessness, I
once saw a report on a tabloid television news magazine
about the unsanitary conditions of our modern hotels. They
reported that even our finer hotels are nothing more than
Petri dishes crawling with the germs that had been spewed
all over the place by previous guests. The reporter used
some sort of dark light which, when shined on items in a
darkened room, revealed where bodily secretions had been
splattered. Traces of humanity in all its liquid and semi solid
forms were found on bedspreads, chairs, floors and even
walls. The report made it clear that almost all hotels were
like this, no matter how high priced the rooms, and no matter
how highly rated by Conde Nast. I wish I had never seen
that show, because ever since watching it I have felt a wave
of nausea wash over me whenever I enter a hotel room.

Despite all this discomfiting knowledge, however, I had
no worries about my room I found after working for Tony.
This is not because the place was as sterile as a surgeon's
scalpel before it slices the flesh. On the contrary, it was the
filthiest place I have ever slept (and I have spent the night in
Winnemucca, Nevada). I was assaulted by grime from the
moment I entered the grandly named O'Farrell Palace. Trash
was strewn across the floor of the lobby and the threadbare
carpet was somehow both dingy with dirt and shiny with
grease. The clerk, who was eating Chinese food from a
small white container, had sweet and sour sauce smeared
across his face from the corner of his mouth almost to his
ear. He was busy "reading" a girlie magazine as I walked to
the desk. Though he no doubt heard me approach, he did not
look up from his reading material. I grunted. Still he
ignored me.

"I want a room," I told him.

He looked at me with an expression of extreme boredom spread across his bovine features. It was a look of apathy that can only be achieved with either a lot of drugs or a very small amount of intelligence. In his case both seemed to apply. "Of course you do," he said, "why else would you be here?"

"You got one?"

"Yessir, especially for you."

I paid him and he handed me the key to a room on the fifth floor. The elevator was out of service, so I had to trudge all the way up (with my underwear biting into my tender area with every step). When I reached my room, I found the key didn't fit the lock and I had to go all the way back down to get another one. The clerk sneered as I explained my predicament. I'm certain he had given me the first key with full knowledge that it didn't work as a sort of prank. Burdened with a new key I trudged back up the staircase and found, (to the great relief of my tortured crotch), that I could now turn the knob.

The room smelled of sweaty bodies and cigarette smoke, but the odor didn't bother me much because I knew I smelled even worse. There was a double bed covered with an orange blanket and I wondered what the television newsmagazine would find smeared across it if they brought their dark light here. I didn't really care though; I was just happy to be indoors. Bodily fluids or no bodily fluids I was going to be sleeping *inside* and *on a bed*. I was gratified to see that there was a television. In fact, there were two, a large one and a small one. The large one, which had apparently stopped working sometime during the Johnson Administration, now served as a table for its smaller companion. The carpet in the room was brown and in a few places it had been worn down to the matting. There was a table and one wooden chair next to the window, but there

131

were neither curtains nor blinds. Instead, a large piece of cardboard was tucked between the table and the wall. The cardboard piece was about the size of the window, and apparently when a patron of the hotel wanted darkness or privacy he had to jam the cardboard into the window frame.

The struggle up and down and up the stairs had taken a lot out of me and I collapsed onto the bed for a moment. I was sweating. After a few minutes I stood up, stripped, and went into the bathroom. It was a tiny little room containing only a sink, shower, toilet, bar of soap, towel and a plastic cup. I turned the shower tap to hot and waited for the warm water to come. It was a long time in coming but when it finally arrived I stepped in and let the soothing cascade run its fingers down my body. The floor of the shower was a suspicious gray color, but I didn't care. The wonderful calming powers of hot water gently pushed all sanitary questions from my mind. I must have spent twenty minutes under the tap. I lathered up my entire body and inhaled the harsh antiseptic odor of cheap soap with pleasure. It had become a sweet smell. I could feel the grime, stench, bacteria and fungus flowing from my body with the water. I paid particular attention to my toes which I lathered up and scrubbed several times. The pain, itch, and irritation of the athlete's foot were almost completely gone.

When I stepped from the shower, I felt new. I was a naked wet baby again. Fresh. I dried myself, wrapped the towel around my waist and went back into the bedroom. I sank into the bed and fell asleep in moments but awoke an hour later, shivering. The room was cold. I put on my new clothes and went out to find some dinner.

I felt better than I had in days. I had money in my pocket, a roof over my head, and, best of all, I was clean. I was a member of the human race again. No one could tell that I was homeless by looking at me. I went to a cheap

Indian restaurant on Larkin Street where I ordered chicken curry and naan. I ate my meal slowly, making sure to mop up every last bit of curry. When I left the restaurant night had deepened and the prostitutes were out in force, and when I arrived at my hotel I discovered that it was a popular place of business with the streetwalkers. The bottom two or three floors, it turned out, were all rented out on an hourly rather than a nightly basis.

But up on the fifth floor all was quiet and I immediately fell into a deep and dreamless sleep.

Chapter 21

I never went back to Tony. When I woke up in an actual bed I was so warm that I just lay there and wallowed in comfort. It wasn't the bed that kept me from going back to Tony though; it was the realization that I wasn't on the street to get a job. The day before had been nice, but it was an aberration. I wasn't doing research on construction work.

When the 11:00 checkout time got close I took another shower and then reluctantly dressed myself and headed back into the street. I wandered downhill to the UN Plaza where I just moped around feeling slightly guilty about letting Tony down. I sat on a bench and, for form's sake, sipped from a bottle of the cheapest vodka I could find. It was called "Uncle Vanya's Premium", and it tasted like wood alcohol. I had never seen Uncle Vanya's for sale in any of the liquor stores in Pacific Heights. They must bottle it in the Tenderloin.

As I warmed up, I watched an old man approach a garbage can and start to dig through its contents. He threw newspapers and takeout containers on the ground as he worked, and the trash piled up around his feet like tailings at the mouth of a mineshaft. He was mining for cans and bottles that he could return for five cents apiece. He found a few, put them in his shopping cart, and then moved on towards the next can as the garbage he had just dug out blew past his ankles in a sudden gust of wind.

As he passed, I studied his features. He had a gaunt and gray-bearded face with red eyes burning from the depths of dark eye sockets. His flat mouth had a gray sludge oozing from the corners, and when it opened I could see that his only tooth was a forlorn canine hanging down like the last stalactite in a dark cave. He was clothed in dirt. Presumably, there was a coat and some pants underneath, but all I could see was that dingy gray/brown coating of dirt. He moved with a twitchy shuffle that wasn't quite a limp and seemed to say that his movements hurt him.

I don't know if it was the Uncle Vanya's taking over, but I was flooded with a feeling of compassion for this man. I wanted to do something for him but was paralyzed by that question that kills so many of the weaker impulses to do a kindness for another human, "What, exactly, should I do?" Give him money? Push his cart for him? Help him dig for cans and bottles? I did what I had done many times before, and I just watched him walk away. I felt a slight ache in my heart as I watched him go, but slight aches in the heart don't help anyone.

As the sun finished setting and only the last deep red glow of the day was still sticking to the low clouds overhead I was hustling change on the corner of Polk and Clay when a man I recognized walked up and dropped some coins into my paper cup with a dry rattling noise.

"I know you," he said.

"Yeah, you told me that story about Haydn. I liked it."

"I have another story. I need somebody to hear it."

"Let's go somewhere we can sit and talk."

We walked three blocks, uphill, to Lafayette Park. Not a single word was exchanged on the way. I glanced at the man who I had come to think of as "the Knifeman," and I could almost see the story boiling inside his head. It was obvious that there was a growing pressure there, and that it needed release.

When we got to the park, we sat on the first bench we came to and he immediately pulled a cigarette out of his pocket and lit it. He sucked the smoke deep into his lungs before blowing it back out through his nostrils. Then he

135

pulled out his knife and snapped it open. He took another deep pull on his cigarette and snapped the knife shut as he blew the smoke out of his mouth. He snapped it open again, and snapped it shut. Snapped open. Snapped shut. He kept on smoking and flicking his knife as he spoke.

"In World War Two the battleships of the United States Navy were named after states; the cruisers were named after cities, the destroyers after people, and the submarines were named after fish. Submarines had names like 'Wahoo', 'Barb', 'Mingo', and 'Tang'. Back then the most dangerous weapons could have the most absurd names. 'Fat Man' and 'Little Boy', for example. But these absurdly named boats sent more Japanese shipping to the bottom of the ocean than any other kind of naval vessel, and the Tang was arguably the greatest of them all, sinking 33 ships for a total of 116,000 tons in her five patrols through Japanese waters.

"On the 24th of September 1944, she stood out to sea for her fifth and final patrol. The Tang sailed from Honolulu to the Formosa Strait where she destroyed every ship she could find. The Tang had left Pearl Harbor carrying twenty-four torpedoes, twelve in her forward torpedo room and twelve more aft. By two-thirty in the morning on October 25th, she had fired twenty-three of them, and she had savaged the Japanese in the process, sinking freighters, tankers, and even a destroyer. She had just one torpedo left and once it had been fired they could turn back to Hawaii for women and beer and a break from the constant looming presence of a dark, cold, and crushing death at the bottom of the ocean.

"From the movies they have seen most people imagine that in World War II submarines spent almost all their time underwater. These days they do, because nuclear reactors make it possible for a sub to stay underwater almost indefinitely, but the Tang ran on diesel engines, and diesel

136

engines need to breathe. At night she would run on the surface, her low profile combining with the darkness to make her almost as invisible as being underwater would have done. She could run her engines and charge her batteries while she was on the surface; she would only flood her ballast tanks and dive if there was danger. During the day she hid under the water using battery power.

"That's why in the early morning darkness on October 25th, 1944 the Tang was running on the surface in the Formosa Strait. Her captain, Richard O'Kane, was commanding from the open-air bridge when he ordered his crew to prepare to fire their last fish. It was a Mark 18 electric torpedo, carrying a powerful 600-pound warhead and capable of swimming through the water at a ripping pace of 29 knots. The Japanese sailors crewing the target, a freighter carrying weapons and food to troops fighting the allies, had no idea how close they were to death as the Tang drew nearer in the darkness.

"The last torpedo to be fired by the Tang swam straight out of its torpedo tube, trailing a phosphorescent wake as it sped through the sea. After about ten seconds, however, the torpedo 'porpoised', popping out of the water erratically before plunging back in. When the torpedo settled down again it was travelling in a wide arc, still churning a phosphorescent glow in its wake, but now it was headed towards the Tang itself. Captain O'Kane could see it all clearly from where he stood on the bridge and he ordered a hard turn under emergency power to avoid that 600 pound warhead, but there's never any escaping fate, and torpedo 24 slammed into the aft torpedo room, killing every sailor inside and immediately flooding it.

"The explosion caused men in the forward areas of the Tang to be thrown into bulkheads so violently that their limbs were broken, while the captain and eight other officers

137

were swept off the bridge and into the sea. The torpedo had caused a mortal wound to the submarine, tearing a hole so big that not only did the aft torpedo room immediately flood, but so did the engine rooms, the motor room, and the maneuvering room, before hatches could be closed to contain the inrushing water.

"The Tang sank stern first. As her rear compartments filled with seawater and plunged downward, her bow was raised high into the air. She was canted at such a steep angle that the floors became walls and the bulkheads became floors as she went down. Broken men with bloodied hands gripped whatever they could to keep themselves from sliding towards the flooded aft compartments. Only one sailor had the opportunity and the speed to climb up the conning tower and jump into the ocean with O'Kane the officers before the Tang disappeared under the waves.

She had left Honolulu with ten officers and sixty-eight enlisted men. Within minutes of the impact of the torpedo, there were only thirty scared survivors left inside the Tang. Other than the few now bobbing in the waves, the rest had all been killed in the blast or drowned almost immediately afterwards.

"When her stern touched the muddy bottom of the strait one of the sailors on board flooded the forward ballast tanks and the Tang settled into the mud with 180 feet of water between her men and the air above. It was then that Japanese destroyers and PT boats began dropping depth charges. The submariners could do nothing but pray as explosions tore through the sea around them. They were in shallow water, unable to move in their damaged vessel, and just waiting for the explosion that would tear open the pressure hull and let in death along with the seawater.

"The pressure hull was not breached, but a fire broke out in the forward battery compartment and spread to the officers' quarters. Soon the air inside the submarine brought a toxic smoky sting to the lungs of all who breathed it.

"The men crowded into the forward torpedo room as the jarring booms of depth charges moved off into the distance. This was the room where their trouble had started, but it was also the only place in the submarine that offered any hope of escape.

"You can't just open a hatch 180 feet below the surface and swim towards life. The hull of a submarine holds the same air pressure that you find at sea level: one standard atmosphere, 14.7 pounds per square inch. The water pressure under 180 feet of water is nearly 80 pounds per square inch. The effects of such a sudden pressure change on a human body are catastrophic. Unsurvivable. But the forward torpedo room contained the submarine's escape locker. Four men could enter the locker, where the pressure would be raised gradually until the air pressure inside that small chamber was the same as the water pressure outside of it. Only then would the locker be flooded, and the men given the chance to escape.

"Four of the thirty survivors climbed into the locker, a hatch closing behind them and leaving them in the darkness. Each of them had a Momsen lung. You shouldn't imagine that a Momsen lung was some kind of scuba tank; it was not. It was a rebreather attached to a bag of air that hadn't been compressed. The main benefit of the Momsen lung was that it scrubbed the carbon dioxide out of the air that the sailors were to breathe and breathe again as they groped towards the surface in the inky obscurity. With every breath they took they would have less oxygen, but at least they wouldn't be poisoned by the carbon dioxide manufactured in their own lungs.

"As these men stood in the dark, close together, breathing the scent of terror oozing out of each other's

139

bodies with their sweat, they could hear depth charges still thumping at what they hoped was a safe distance. The process of increasing the air pressure was uncomfortable, painful even, to the men who were preparing to escape. And as they stood there, suffering, their minds ran into thoughts of what would happen to them on the surface, assuming they were still alive when they got there. There were three options: nobody would see them and they would die of thirst or drowning, they would be captured by the Japanese and interrogated before being beheaded and tossed back into the water to feed the sharks, or they would be taken prisoner and spend the rest of the war in prison camps. By 1944 everybody already knew how the Japanese treated the prisoners in their camps.

"Soon these men were banging on the hatch. They had changed their minds. They didn't want to go to the surface. Even though staying on the submarine meant death, it was preferable to their imagined alternatives.

"Another batch of four men took their place in the escape locker, and these four suffered the same pains and fears as the first four, but they stuck it out, feeling the pain in their ears and joints as their bodies attempted to deal with the change in pressure, thinking dark thoughts about their futures. Then the air pressure became equal to the water pressure, and these four men were released into the water 180 feet below the waves.

"A small buoy attached to the Tang by a knotted rope had been released. The buoy bobbed unnoticed on the surface of the water as Japanese patrol boats continued to search the area. One hundred and eighty feet below that buoy four men grabbed the rope and began to follow it to the surface. Their instincts doubtless told them to swim upward as hard and fast as they could, but their training told them to go slow because the sudden change in pressure from 80 pounds per square inch to just 14.7 would kill them just as surely as the change in the other direction would have. Too rapid an ascent would cause their blood to fizz, it would destroy their blood vessels, it would lead to massive internal bleeding and death. They were to follow that rope, pause where it was knotted, count for thirty seconds, and then ascend to the next knot. All this was done in perfect darkness, with depth charges still thumping, sending shockwaves through the water as they stood still at a knot in the rope.

"That night 13 men got into the escape locker and attempted to reach the surface. Some of them disappeared somewhere between the Tang and the air, others reached the surface, but had come up too quickly and died. Five survived to be rescued by the Japanese who turned them over to the crew of a ship they had sunk earlier that night to be beaten. Then they were hauled off to POW camps. Including the officers who survived after being knocked off the deck and the sailor who climbed up the conning tower, a total of nine men survived the destruction of the Tang."

The Knifeman's cigarette had burned out halfway through his story and he quickly lit another. As he drew the smoke into his lungs I imagined that it tasted almost as sweet to him as that first breath of fresh air on the surface had tasted to the survivors of the Tang. Once his blood had been calmed by the infusion of nicotine he spoke, "My story has a twist. I'll bet you can't guess what it is."

I thought I had a pretty good idea what the twist might be, but something told me to keep it to myself, "What's the twist?"

"They were robots. All of them. Captain O'Kane, the officers, the enlisted men, Franklin Delano Roosevelt and even Emperor Hirohito. Robots. All of them." Having

141

revealed his twist, the Knifeman tossed his cigarette on the ground and wandered off into the night.

Chapter 23

San Francisco is a pretty good city for private detectives. This is Sam Spade's hometown, after all, a place of shadows and fog. Any city with a lot of money has a lot of things that bear looking into, and it's detectives who often do that looking. Even so, I'd never actually met a private detective before.

It pains me to admit it, but all my favorite fictional detectives are from Los Angeles. Sam Spade is just not as good as Philip Marlowe. I like Marlowe for his toughness, his brains, and the incorruptibility that belies his corrupted demeanor. I like how he says cynical things like, "She gave me a smile I could feel in my hip pocket," and "From 30 feet away she looked like a lot of class. From 10 feet away she looked like something made up to be seen from 30 feet away," but also poetic things like, "I was as hollow and empty as the spaces between stars." (I can almost hear Neil DeGrasse Tyson clearing his throat as he prepares to object to the last quote, but Chandler was writing in more innocent times when we knew nothing about dark matter or dark energy.)

I was on my way to see a private detective, the first one I would ever meet in the flesh. The noir detectives from the 40s never did any divorce work, but the detective I was about to see, Roland P. Proctor, wasn't so shy about destroying families. Right there on his website where he listed the sort of work he could do for his clients, "divorce" was at the top in bold letters. Underneath "divorce" was the service I wanted, "missing persons." Now, you might argue that Abby was not missing at all. She was exactly where she wanted to be, and everyone she cared about, presumably, knew where she was. But as far as I was concerned, she was missing, and I hoped that Roland P. Proctor would see things my way.

Mr. Proctor had an office in a building on the corner of Leavenworth and Turk, one of the most unsavory corners in the entire city. Since becoming homeless I had spent a lot of time in the Tenderloin. I fit in a lot better there than I did in Pacific Heights or Nob Hill, and there is a sort of comfort in being where you fit in, even if that place is seedy, awful smelling, crime ridden, filthy, and degenerate. But even as a homeless person Turk Street was a bit much. It's a murdery strip of road with used hypodermic needles scattered across the pavement like confetti after a ticker tape parade.

Proctor was not what I had expected of a private detective. First of all, he was a large man, physically unsuited for sneaking about. It is important for you to understand that when I say "large" I am not implying that he was muscular. He was large in a very soft and round way. He didn't look physically capable of performing the duties of a private detective as I understood them. For example, I couldn't imagine this puffy man laying into a recalcitrant witness with a blackjack or the knuckle dusters. He was bald and had a shaved head, but he was not bald in the way that, say Vin Diesel or The Rock are bald. Action movie heroes are somehow able to make their bald heads look like powerful extra muscles. Proctor's bald head, on the other hand, was fat and soft, like an overripe peach. He was wearing a gray tee shirt that had clearly been manufactured with a much smaller man in mind, and his greasy, loose flesh oozed out of it at the sleeves, collar and belly. After opening the door and stepping aside so that I could enter his one room office (unlike movie detectives, Proctor did not have a sexy/sassy secretary/girl-Friday to let me in) he walked back behind his desk and slumped into a chair that made a wail of complaint as it was crushed beneath his mountainous girth.

His office was a wreck. Newspapers were scattered around, mixed with what appeared to be files relating to his cases and eight by twelve photographs of husbands and wives being caught in compromising situations that would allow their spouses to grind them to a fine powder in the divorce. There was a computer from the 90s sitting in one corner, covered with dust. It had apparently been placed there over a decade ago when Proctor had installed the newer, but already ancient, machine that now sat on his desk, also covered with dust, although not quite as much. He had motivational posters on the walls, the kinds of posters that say things like "Motivation: it's what the future is made of" and have a stock photograph of a one legged man climbing a mountain.

Proctor saw the way I was studying his office and he said, by way of explanation but without embarrassment, "People don't usually come to my office; they just call me on the phone or shoot me an email."

"Yeah," I said as I nodded my head, agreeing that it was probably for the best that as few of his clients as possible saw him or his office.

"Well, what can I do for you?" he asked, as he held up a camcorder that looked even older than his computers, "Need me to make some videos of your wife for the divorce?" He had a disgustingly lewd sort of smile on his face as he asked this question.

"No. I'm not married."

"You want evidence of your girlfriend cheating?" he said with fading hope.

"Also, no. I want to find a missing person."

"A girl?"

"A woman, yes."

"What was her last known address?"

"I don't know."

145

"You got a picture?"

"No."

"Have you gone to the police?"

"Well, no, you see, the truth is, she's not really 'missing,' it's just that I want to find her."

The leer bloomed back across his face, "Ah, a stalker job."

"A… a what!?"

"Stalker job. Not so unusual. Nothing to be ashamed of. You have a girl you like, she's hiding from you, and you want to find her so you can stalk her. Fine. I'm good at that but I do have a legal document I need to you to sign." I was too flabbergasted to defend my motives as he rummaged through his desk for a moment before pulling out a single sheet of paper and handing it to me. The paper said:

INDEMNITY

I _____ (Client) have hereby hired the estimable Roland P. Proctor (Proctor) to find _____ (Findee) and I certify that I have engaged Proctor for purposes that are entirely legal. I hereby warrant that I do not intend to kidnap, murder, rape/murder, grope, invade the privacy of, or send threatening love letters to, the Findee. In the event that Findee becomes deceased under mysterious circumstances or brings charges of any kind against Proctor, Client agrees to Indemnify Proctor for any and all damages including damages for pain, suffering, and emotional distress, and

146

to confess to the murder or other crimes
perpetrated against the Findee while
leaving Proctor's name out of it.

"You just sign it right there," he said helpfully.

I was finally shaken out of my stupor and spluttered, "What is this awful document?"

"Look, I'm not going to judge you, and I'm not going to pretend that I'm somehow above doing a stalker job, but I've been bitten by these deals in the past so I need you to sign the release."

"I'm not a stalker!"

"Sure, sure you're not a stalker. Of course not. But I just need to make sure I have my bases covered for when you get caught in the bushes outside her house and the cops want to know how you tracked her down."

"But I'm not going to be in the bushes!"

"Of course not. But I had a guy tell me that once, and then the girl I found for him went missing for real, and the cops somehow traced it back to me and they had a lotta questions. Luckily, things turned out okay."

"She turned up safe?"

"No. They never found her body, so they didn't have enough evidence to bring charges against anybody. But now I gotta be careful, so, just sign the agreement."

"Look, you've got this all wrong. I met a girl, we really clicked, but before I could get her number we were separated by circumstances."

"Ahh, so it's not a stalker job, it's a star-crossed lovers job."

"Exactly!"

"I'm sorry, but 'star crossed lover' is just another way of saying 'stalker'. You want me to find her, then you gotta sign the release."

147

Well, when he put it that way it really clarified things for me. I did not want this man to find Abby for me. I wanted him to stay as far away from her as possible. The thought of this disgusting man breathing the same air as Abby made me sick and I wouldn't have it. I gave him an insincere, "I'm sorry I wasted your time," and then stormed out of his office.

Chapter 24

One good thing about being homeless is that you can do it anywhere. Well, almost anywhere. Obviously, you can't do it in a home. And, also obviously, you can't do it in many parks after dark, or inside businesses, or on benches where they have installed anti-homeless spikes. The more I think about it, the more I realize how circumscribed the life of a homeless person is. What I wanted to say, really, was that if you are homeless, you can go where you want, when you want, and do what you want when you get there, as long as it doesn't cost much money or make normal people with homes uncomfortable. The key thing is that you are outside the grip of a job, and if you want to sit across the street from the Hunan Burrito in the hopes of seeing the girl you love and tailing her back to her home so she can never escape from you again, you have the necessary time at your disposal.

I realize how this sounds. Clearly, I need to spend more effort on thinking before I shove words onto the paper, because I worry I'm giving you some wrong idea. I'm a good guy. That's the important thing to remember. I've never been a stalker before, and despite the words I had exchanged with Proctor I still didn't consider myself a 'stalker'. I wasn't a stalker. I was a man in love who had the misfortune of not knowing where the woman he was in love with lived. Granted, I didn't know where she lived because she hadn't told me, but I think if you really look into your heart you will see that there are extenuating circumstances that make my behavior acceptable.

You may ask, "Instead of waiting for Abby in front of Hunan Burrito and then following her home, like some kind of creep, if she passes by and you are lucky enough to see

149

her, why don't you just walk up to her, chirp a jaunty 'hello' in her direction, and procure her phone number by honest means?" This is a reasonable question, and it has a reasonable answer. I didn't want to reintroduce myself to her at the moment because I was disgusting and dirty from living on the streets. I smelled like a homeless person. I looked like one. I needed to avoid her at all cost for the time being, but I also had to figure out where I could find her for when I was prepared (showered, coiffed, starched, cologned) to accidentally run into her just outside of her apartment or workplace.

But first, I had to find her. My experience with Proctor had made me decide to give up on private detectives. If Abby was going to be found, I would have to do the finding myself, and the only idea I had for locating Abby was to camp out in front Hunan Burrito, in that gray area where the Financial District blurs into Chinatown, and hope that she came back. She had mentioned something about frequently walking by the restaurant, so even if she never went back there to eat, I might catch a glimpse of her walking by. If she walked by, I was going to tail her.

Again, even as I write that last sentence, I realize how ugly it sounds. Just look at me, I was a dramatically disheveled man who had admitted to being inordinately attracted to Asian women, and now I intended to "tail" one of them. I know that this looks bad, and as you read it you are probably arching a disapproving eyebrow and muttering "gross."

I set my backpack on the ground against the wall of a dry cleaners across the street from Hunan Burrito, and I settled in to watch. I pulled my hat down low over my eyes and hoped that the low hat would combine with my beard and my homeless man's garb to make me invisible to Abby if she passed by. People generally try to avoid looking directly at homeless men. Eye contact can lead to a plea for money or a confrontation. I had all the camouflage necessary to blend into the urban jungle.

At first, I felt a strange exhilaration created by the knowledge that I could see Abby at any moment. Since she passed this way often, she could be close. She could be within five hundred feet of me right now, working in an office or cubicle. Graphic designing up a storm. Was it possible that she could be thinking of me at that this moment? That was probably too much to hope for. But had she thought of me even once since our meeting in that not-very-good restaurant across the street?

This was my first stakeout, and I was not prepared for the tedium of it. I had hurried over to a spot in front of Hunan Burrito right after my meeting with Proctor and I was in place by 10:30. The initial feeling of exhilaration only lasted about ten minutes before I started to notice that I wasn't quite as comfortable as I would have liked; it was a bit cold, and I was bored. Bored, bored, bored. So bored. There's nothing worse than reading about how bored somebody is, but I need you to know I was bored. I was so bored. Bored. Bored. Booooooooored. So bored.

Fifteen minutes passed.

Then fifteen more.

It was 11:00 now. I had seen stakeouts in cop movies and they always looked kind of fun. Just sitting in your warm car shootin' the breeze with another cop while you drink coffee and smoke cigarettes and listen to a ballgame on the radio. The length of the stakeout could be measured by the size of the cigarette butt pile. But I don't smoke so there was no way to measure the progress I was making.

By 11:30 I wanted to leave. I mean, how could I know if she was even going to come by? I was sitting out there in the cold with no guarantee that I would ever see her walk down this street today, or any other day. It was possible that I was wasting my time. Probable even. But still I stayed. This was my only chance. My only idea for ever seeing her again. My love was more powerful than cold, boredom, and mild discomfort.

But desperation drove me to think. Was this really the only option? What did I know about Abby? Well, her name was Abigail and she was a graphic designer. Couldn't I find her with those two details? Couldn't I look up all graphic design firms in the immediate vicinity of Hunan Burrito and find out if any of them employed an Abigail? I could! And I would! I was about to give up on the whole stakeout concept and dedicate myself to this new plan when I heard a voice.

"Daniel?"

It was her. Abigail. In the flesh. The lovely flesh. I glanced up at her for a moment, doubtless with a look of total shock on my face. I had assumed that I would see her first, be unrecognized by her, and then be able to follow her to wherever she was going so I'd know where to find her later. But now here she was. She had found me first. Me. Dirty, filthy, stinky, me. In my stained coat and stained pants. With black grime under my fingernails. With my greasy beard. And, worst of all, maybe looking a bit like I was lying in wait for her.

It's weird to be in love and to feel your heart soar at the sight of the one you love, while also feeling your heart crash and auger into the swamp because you know you are disgusting and being caught at a bad, bad moment. For a moment I considered pretending that I wasn't Daniel. That I had never heard of Daniel. That it was foolishness bordering on insanity for her to call me by this name. But almost immediately I saw that this plan wouldn't work, so I put on a smile and said, "Abby?"

152

"I thought that was you, but you look…"

I could see she was struggling to find a polite way to describe how I looked, so I helped her out, "Like a filthy bum?"

She laughed, "Something like that. I wouldn't have put it in those words exactly."

"Well, they're the right words. I can own it. Remember how I told you I was going to be homeless to research my book?"

"Oh! That makes sense! But, should I talk to you? I don't know what the procedure is. If somebody from your not homeless world talks to you, does that take you out of the moment or anything?"

"Not at all. Let's talk."

"Would it be all right if we ate lunch together? It could be like a good Samaritan thing you could use in your novel. I want to hear about your experiences. We can go to Hunan Burrito for old times' sake."

Let's just pause and take a look at the four sentences immediately preceding this one to admire how glorious they are. First of all, did you notice that she asked me out on a date? You might argue that it's not really a date, that we just ran into each other at lunchtime so of course we would eat together, as friendly acquaintances. But stop being such a downer! It was a date! Never in my wildest fantasies had I imagined that my stakeout would lead directly to a date and that she would be the one asking for it. Next, well, the second sentence isn't that great. If anything, it seems to turn the lunch invitation into an act of charity, so let's ignore it and go on to the third sentence. She wanted to hear about my experiences! She wanted to listen to me! Unless you are interested in a person, listening to that person is usually unpleasant work. At the very least this third sentence proved that she was interested in me. Yes, yes, I know. Not

153

necessarily "romantically" interested, but at this stage any kind of interest was welcome. And finally, that last sentence clearly shows that in her mind we already had a history together. You can't have an old times sake if you haven't already had some times. All this was good.

I just wished that I didn't smell so bad. Still, I accepted her offer, assuring her that a good Samaritan chapter was just what my novel needed.

We took a seat near the window and I tried to lean back as far away as I could so she wouldn't smell the funk that was coming from my body. She noticed what I was doing right away and laughed, "Are you trying to keep away from me so I don't have to smell you?"

"Yes."

"Don't worry about it! You smell pretty good, all things considered. Now tell me all about what you have been up to."

And I did, omitting, of course, any mention of Roland P. Proctor. And as far as I could tell she hung on my every word. There is nothing more gratifying to a man's vanity than to have a beautiful woman hang on his every word. But we weren't here so that I could gratify my vanity. We were here so that I could get her phone number, and I now made the attempt. This was a tricky operation fraught with peril. When a girl already has a boyfriend you can't just say "give me your number" because she will instantly hold her boyfriend up as a shield to fend off your request, even if, as I hoped was true in this case, she actually wants to give you her number. You have to devise a bogus reason to get it. I launched the best one I could come up with. It was weak, but I hoped it would be enough.

"Anyway, if you'd like, since you seem interested in it, I could share my novel with you once I've written it. Give me your number and we can keep in touch." Since I had no

154

phone, she had to write it down in the notebook where I had been keeping a journal of my experiences. I was in such a good mood that even the arrival of my extraordinarily mediocre Mongolian beef and fried rice burrito couldn't dampen my spirits.

When there was a lull in the conversation I sent up a flair in an attempt to illuminate the lay of the land, "I'm expecting Chad to show up at any minute with his book of short stories."

She laughed, "I don't think you have to worry about that." The flair produced at best a dim light. She hadn't said anything explicit, but I sensed from her tone that they were still together. I don't know why I had expected them to have broken up. I suppose it was the illogical hope of a man caught in a crush.

When you're eating dinner with a woman you like, particularly in a first date kind of scenario (which I insist this was, despite possible naysaying from any contrarians who might happen to see this manuscript), there is a pivotal moment that occurs at the end of the meal. When both parties have finished eating there is a sort of pause. If one member of the pair isn't enjoying the company of the other, that person will usually make an immediate move to leave the table. The bill will be called for, a plate will be pushed pointedly away, a coat will be put on, or maybe a credit card will be extracted from a wallet. All this will serve as a signal that seems to say, "I am done. I want to get back to the part of my day where I'm not spending any time with you."

I finished my burrito before Abby finished hers. (When I say "finished" I don't mean that I ate all of it. I just mean that I reached a point where I couldn't face another bite of Chinese food in a tortilla and I had to abandon the burrito on my plate like a shark-gnawed mariner whose body has been allowed to drift onto deserted beach.) I watched as she continued to work on her burrito, taking careful feminine bites, making sure she didn't smear sauce on her cheeks or chin. I was waiting for that moment when she would finish.

To my astonishment, she ate her entire burrito. Then she wiped her beautiful mouth with a napkin (even though it was perfectly clean) before proceeding with the conversation as if she hadn't noticed that the eating portion of our lunch had concluded. "Do you want me to give you a tip?" she asked.

"A tip?"

"Yeah, for making more money when you're panhandling."

"I would love a tip."

"You need a dog. These days people still love dogs, but they don't seem to care that much about humans."

"You're onto something."

"The best would be a real sad looking mutt, with only three legs if you can find one. A clinically depressed dog with only three legs is the ideal. Women love a man with a three-legged dog. Shows he has compassion."

"I'm not trying to pick up women at the moment."

"No, but women will give money to a guy with a three-legged dog, a sad one. I promise you."

"Well, I am on peternity leave."

"The only thing better than a three-legged dog would be a two-legged dog, with a set of wheels replacing the missing back legs. If you find a dog like that, I'll give you all my money."

"How much longer are you going to live on the street?"

"Oh, another week or so I guess. When it's over I'll take a hot shower for so long that the California Department of

Water Resources will panic as they notice the water supply noticeably begin to dip, and then I'll collapse into my soft bed and sleep for at least twenty hours straight."

"I can't believe you're actually going through with it. When you told me that you were going to research your book by living on the street, I sort of assumed it was just braggadocio."

"Ohhhh, I see, you thought I was a liar. You know. In the old days I would have had no choice to but to challenge you to a duel."

"Oh no you wouldn't have. In the old days, my opinion wouldn't have mattered because I'm a woman, and I did *not* call you a liar. I was just saying that I didn't think you'd be able to stick it."

"Ah, so I'm not a liar, I'm weak."

"Stop turning everything I say around!" she shouted as she gave me a playful punch to the shoulder. This was the first time that there had ever been any sort of contact between us, and it sent a buzz through my body. I know it was just a punch, but I'm telling you it was an electric one. "All I'm saying is, that it seems like a really hard thing to do, and I'm very impressed. There, does that satisfy your fragile male ego?"

"Nothing will ever satisfy the male ego, but the male ego appreciates the effort."

"What's the worst part about living on the streets?"

I almost told her "not being with you" which would have been accurate, but not the right answer at all at the moment. Sometimes the true answer isn't the correct one. Instead I said, "Well, it changes. At first, the worst thing was being scared to fall asleep in the Tenderloin at night. I couldn't fall asleep because I was afraid I would be attacked. Then the worst part was cold, then the worst part was hunger, then the worst part was being bored, then the worst part was

157

being looked down on as trash by everyone, then the worst part was being wet, then the worst part was getting a terrible case of athlete's foot."

"What has surprised you about it?"

"How some things don't change. I'm still me, essentially, on the street or not. I still have the same emotions, think about the same things, and the same people."

"Oh," she said with a sly smile, suspecting, correctly, that I was referring to her, "what people?"

"Gary Coleman mostly."

She laughed, and as she laughed I said, with my heart thumping in my chest like a man trying to stomp the mud off his boots, "I've been thinking about you too a bit, to be honest."

"Oh really?"

"We really hit it off the other day, didn't we?"

"Yes. We did. I don't think I've ever felt a feeling of friendship bloom that quickly before."

I wasn't sure how to take the word "friendship." Some would say that when a girl drops the f-word, it is a polite way of derailing romantic aspirations. It was disheartening, but I didn't let it bring me down.

"Books are bridges," I said.

"I've said the same thing. You know, you have a way of always bringing things back to books."

"I don't usually, but it seems right with you. You're as bookish as I am, and books are an endless field of common ground that we can travel together, forever."

"Books can be barriers too."

"I know it. I use them as barriers all the time."

"They can close you off from other people. They can reduce you to an observer, like someone who spends all day scrolling through Facebook or Instagram. Not quite as tacky, but essentially the same. Always observing, and never living."

"You're right. I fall into that sometimes. The last few weeks have brought me out of it. Violently." I scrutinized her face as I said this, but I couldn't tell if she had caught my implication. "But we can fall into ruts without books too."

"That's true, for sure. I've fallen into ruts without the help of books... I'd better get back to work." She seemed legitimately reluctant to leave. "Will you get in touch with me when you've got a draft of your novel? I'd like to read it."

"Of course. I'd like to read your book some time as well."

She gave me a noncommittal nod, stood, touched my shoulder, said "goodbye," and walked out of Hunan Burrito.

159

Chapter 25

After Abigail left, I sat perfectly still for a while, basking in the remnants of her warm glow. I didn't want to shake it off. If I moved even an inch the happiness that covered me might be sloughed off. All I wanted to do was sit there and enjoy the buzz that being with her had given me. I stared blankly into space with a slight smile curled up on my lips like a purring cat on a windowsill. I didn't immediately notice when somebody, an enormous person, walked into the restaurant and sat at my table.

It was Roland P. Proctor, and he had rested the burden of his onerous bulk on a cheap plastic chair that didn't look like it was up to the task of supporting him. It was the chair Abigail had vacated only a minute before. It irked me to think that her body had probably left some of its warmth on that seat, and now his body was soaking it up. "What are you doing here?" I asked him. "Did you follow me?"

He didn't answer, instead he asked a question of his own, "What's your book about?"

He paused, giving me a chance to respond. I didn't take it. Then he spoke again, "I'll bet it's about her, that sexy little number who just left, am I right?"

I glared at him.

"I'll bet that's the girl you were going to pay me to find, isn't it? You're a plucky little guy, I'll give you that. It only took you a couple hours to find her yourself after you stormed out of my office on your high horse."

"What do you want?"

"I want to tell you about my novel. Do you want to know what it's about?"

"No."

"It's about blackmail." He paused again, letting the ugly word settle over the table like the ominous darkness of a solar eclipse.

"Are you making some kind of threat?"

"Of course not. I'm just telling you about my novel. Isn't that what polite people do? Talk about their novels?"

"I have no idea what polite people do, and I'm sure you don't either."

He chuckled, "You're pretty uppity for a stalker."

"I am not…"

He cut me off, "Whoa! I told you before, I don't care. Do whatever you want! Stalk up a storm! I'm not going to judge you; I'm just here to tell you about my novel."

"The one about blackmail?"

"Yeah. That's the one."

"I've read a lot of books with blackmailers in them. Nobody likes them. They tend to get killed a lot."

He chucked again, "If I didn't know better, I'd say you were the one making threats now. There's no reason for anybody to make threats. Nobody is going to get killed; just let me tell you about my book. It will interest you. I promise."

I didn't respond and he ploughed ahead, "It's about this guy who comes into the office of a private detective. This detective is, I'll admit, a bit of a shady kind of a character. He's good at his job, but he's not the kind of guy you want to put a lot of trust in, because he's always looking out for number one. If you invite him over for dinner, you're going to want to count the spoons after he leaves.

"So, this guy wants the detective to find a girl. A real hot one, by the way. Very nice." He winked at me. "But him and the detective don't see eye to eye on everything and the guy leaves. But the detective, well, he hasn't worked in two weeks. That's how the business is, feast or famine.

That's why the detective has an office on Turk. He's under appreciated. Underutilized. Underfunded. Well, I don't have to tell you that when a guy hasn't had a legit job in a while his financial situation starts to look sorta iffy, and he has to scrap around a little bit. And, since he's not doing anything else, the detective has the time to scrap around.

"So, this detective, he decides to shadow the guy who was just in his office. Maybe see what he's up to. Stalkers are never up to anything good, and maybe he'll see something that will give him a chance to put the bite on the guy. Well, the guy walks down to Chinatown and sets up shop across from a horrible looking Mexican-Chinese fusion restaurant. It takes the detective a minute to realize that the guy is staking the place out, but the guy is an amateur, no idea what he's doing, and it's all pretty obvious to the detective. Well, the detective has nothing else going on, so he steps into the coffee shop next door to the Mexican-Chinese place, gets a table by the window and settles into watch his erstwhile client.

"By the way, do you know what 'erstwhile' means? I just learned it this morning and I've been looking for a chance to try it out all day. It means 'former.' I got a little calendar on my desk with the word of the day on it. You learn a new vocabulary word every single day. That's 365 new words every year. You know, self-improvement is important to me. You can use 'erstwhile' in your book if you want. It's a nice ten cent word. I'm gonna use it in mine for sure.

"Anyway. So, eventually this Korean girl shows up. A real looker, and classy too. And she says something to the guy. The detective thinks 'uh oh, this is the girl,' and he waits for her to light into the guy. The detective rubs his hands and thinks, 'oh boy, get ready for the fireworks.' Girls don't like getting stalked and she's gonna be

162

maaaaaaad. But to his surprise she doesn't seem to hate the guy. She's not afraid of him. She's not mad at him. They talk. They smile. And then, it blows the detective's mind, but it happens, the two go into that lousy restaurant and eat a couple Chinese burritos together, laughing and talking the whole time."

"Like I said. All of this surprises the detective. He realizes the guy isn't a stalker. He was telling the truth. And the detective almost gives up on the idea of putting the bite on the guy, but something seems off about the whole situation. Why did the guy try to hire the detective in the first place? The detective, he doesn't know all the details, and, frankly, he doesn't care, but he guesses that if the girl was to find out that the guy had hired a detective to find her, it would be bad for him. What do you think, would it be bad for him?

All I could do was scowl in response.

"It would. So, the detective tells the guy he's gotta cough up a thousand bucks or the detective will tell the cute little Korean girl everything."

I finally spoke, "This is blackmail! A felony! I'm going to tell the police and you'll rot in prison."

"Hey! Whoa! Blackmail? We're just talking about a novel here. It's just fiction. I just wanted to give you a chance to decide how the story ends. Should I make it a happily ever after? Come to my office by Saturday at the latest and let me know how it's gonna end. Bring a thousand bucks when you come. One thing about the story though, we all know the guy won't go to the cops, because then the girl will find out about the detective for sure. And the cops won't do anything anyway, because it's just a story between friends. A bit of fiction. So the guy will either bring the money on Saturday, or else he will lose the girl. Anyway.

Think about it and let me know how you think it should end.

Proctor left, and I went back to staring blankly into space, but the warm glow of love was long gone.

Chapter 26

That night I was awakened at two AM by what I initially assumed was the sound of fighting cats. There was a lot of hissing, yowling, screaming and scratching. It was an ugly, grating, unpleasant assortment of noises. But as I listened, I gradually became aware that the sounds I was hearing were not feline, but human. One voice belonged to a male, and the other to a female. I strained my ear to hear what they were screaming at one another. She was angry at him because he was not letting her sleep in a box which, she insisted, they had discovered as a team. She pointed out that she was his woman, and he therefore had a duty to care for her. He screamed back that she had nothing to do with the discovery of the box, and, in any case, there was not enough room for her. She took this to mean that he thought she was fat and the tone of her screaming, which had already been quite shrill, went up an octave. I shouted at them to shut up, outdoing both of them for shrillness, but they ignored me and continued their howling until about an hour later when they both lost their voices. They apparently made up because the next morning I spotted a large refrigerator box at the mouth of the alley with a total of four legs sticking out of the bottom of it.

I miss my walls. Philip Larkin wrote, "We all hate home And having to be there: I detest my room, It's specially-chosen junk, The good books, the good bed, And my life, in perfect order." But right now, I love my home, and more than anything else would like to spend a night in that good bed. I've always been a soft bed kind of guy. Some people want their mattresses to be stiff boards, but not me. I'm not going to use my mattress preference to show off how tough I am. I like to sleep on a soft, downy, pillow-like sort of mattress, a mattress that seems to hug me, to swallow me in warmth and comfort. I've had nothing but concrete in days, and I am over it.

Chapter 27

I had spent five hours panhandling and the rest of the day sitting around Mission Dolores Park. That's what my research boiled down to. Sitting around. I had read the newspaper, listened to a hippy strum Jefferson Airplane songs badly on a battered acoustic guitar, and watched a group of twenty somethings play ultimate Frisbee while keeping one eye on the ground at all times in an effort to avoid the dog turds scattered across the grass like painted eggs on Easter morning.

As I sat on the grass below the cement path that bisects the park I watched a woman struggling to push a shopping cart full of her filthy belongings across the grass on the field below. The cart was heavy and had not been built to be pushed through grass. She struggled to move it. One of the frisbee players jogged over and grabbed the front of the cart, clearly with the intention of helping her, but she screamed at him and he sheepishly jogged back to his game. The park seemed cruelly wide as I watched her shabby metal boat transverse that sea of green, and by the time she reached the sidewalk on the other side I was reminded that I wasn't really experiencing the life of a street person.

I'm not a drug addict and I don't have mental problems. If I had been pushing that cart and somebody tried to help me, I would have let them. It was hard for me to imagine what life might be like for her, fearing and distrusting strangers who so obviously didn't mean her any harm. I wouldn't ever be able to understand that woman. The best I could do was guess at what went on in her mind. It depressed me a little to consider how hopeless my research project was. Yes, I was begging and sleeping on the streets at night. But I wasn't having the same experience she was. I

167

wasn't even close. She lad layers and layers of problems that I couldn't simulate. I knew that homelessness would end for me soon, while for her, there was no hope in sight. She would be pushing that cart around until she died, or went to jail, or became so sick she had to be institutionalized. I was having a good time, relatively speaking, sitting in the park, reading, sipping on a little bottle of Uncle Vanya's, watching the parade of life pass in front of me. But I doubted that any part of that woman's life could be considered a good time.

Dusk came, and then darkness. Not that the city is ever truly dark. The marine layer seems to come closer and to lower itself over the city as night comes on, and all the electric light radiated by civilization is reflected back to it. San Francisco glows at night. The park was almost deserted now, and I was sitting alone on the grass while the scent of marijuana wafted over me from somewhere nearby. I was making my mind up to go find something to eat when a man appeared out of the glowing darkness and sat on the grass a few feet away.

I recognized his slightly twitching face immediately, even in the dim light. He was the Knifeman, the man who had smoked and played with his knife as he told me the stories of Joseph Haydn's missing head and the sinking of the Tang.

He didn't say anything to me for a while. Instead, he drew a cigarette from his package of Camels and lit it with his Zippo. He pulled the smoke deeply into his lungs, making the tip of his cigarette burn hot and bright for a moment, before letting the smoke escape him like his soul leaving his body. The Knifeman made a slight hum of satisfaction and then pulled his pocketknife out of his pocket. He flicked the blade out, and snapped it shut. Flipped the blade out, and snapped it shut again. He seemed

168

more jittery, more on edge, than the last time I had seen him, and the knife flicking made me more nervous than it had before.

"I know you," he said.

"Yeah, you've told me a couple of your stories."

"I have a new story. I need to tell it."

"I'd like to hear it."

"It's about a woman named Winifred. Although in the novel I will mostly refer to her by her title, Lady Nithsdale, out of respect, because she was an impressive woman. A one in a million woman. I often think that if I'd had a woman like her in my corner I could have done anything. Anything. Instead I just wander around in the dark telling my stories and smoking."

"Nobody seems to be named Winifred anymore."

"No. It's an old-fashioned name. Dignified."

"You could call her Winnie."

"No, not her. Winnie isn't enough name for her. She was Lady Nithsdale," he said as he flicked his knife decisively open.

"She was a real person?"

The knife snapped shut. "Of course. As real as you or me."

I wasn't entirely convinced that the Knifeman was real, but I thought it best to keep this thought to myself. "What is your story about?" I asked.

He took an extra deep pull on his cigarette, like a diver taking a big breath before plunging into dark water in search of a pearl, then he spoke as smoke flowed out of his mouth with his words, "Queen Anne died in 1714, the last of the Stuarts to rule Britain, and she was succeeded by a German prince, George, the Elector of Hanover. There were over fifty people who had a better claim to the throne, but all of them were Roman Catholics, and the British were done with popish kings. George wasn't a particularly likable slab of beef and having a German for a king wasn't something that set well with many Britons, but he took the throne as the best of a bad lot.

"There were those who thought that the king should be a Stuart, and they had a candidate at hand: James, Queen Anne's half-brother. These supporters of the Stuart claim were called the Jacobites. They were mostly Catholic and they were based in Scotland and the north of England, so it was in the north that they raised an army for the purpose of imposing Stuart rule by force. They believed that, with a little pressure, support for the fat and gouty German who had been so wrongly seated on the throne would collapse. The people would flock to their standard. But the people still remembered how much they had hated James II, and they didn't want his Catholic son. The Jacobite army was a little band of 4,000 men as it marched south, and it did not swell into an irrepressible multitude.

"These soldiers met the King's redcoats in battle at the town of Preston, in Lancashire. The fighting was house to house, with each army trying to burn the other out of the town. In the end, the Jacobites were no match for the redcoats, and they were forced to surrender. The six noblemen who had led them were taken prisoner and brought south for trial and execution. They were locked up in the Tower of London while they awaited their fates.

"William Maxwell, 5th Earl of Nithsdale, and the husband of Winifred, Lady Nithsdale, was one of those men.

"When she heard news of the battle, Lady Nithsdale didn't hesitate. She was not daunted by the cold of late December or the once in a century blizzard that had struck Britain and buried it under a blanket of snow. She headed out on horseback and rode hard to the South, never knowing if she would arrive to find her husband's head already separated from his body and spiked to some wall where it would serve as a warning to the enemies of King George.

"When she arrived in London she learned that her husband had not been tried yet. But he soon was, and he was found guilty.

"The king had the power to pardon, and it wasn't impossible to imagine that a wise king might choose to purchase popularity with a grand demonstration of forgiveness and mercy. But the king wasn't in a merciful mood, and when Lady Nithsdale put all her pride aside and threw herself at his feet, clutching him by his silk swaddled knees and begging him to pardon her husband, he made desperate attempts to disengage her from his person and then had her dragged away. Her husband was not pardoned.

"The Tower of London had already attained its fearsome reputation by then. It was in the Tower that Anne Boleyn, as she waited her death, famously said, "I heard say the executioner was very good, and I have a little neck," (the knife flicked out) and it was there that her head was stuck off with a sword (the knife flicked shut). It was in the Tower that another of Henry VIII's wives, Catherine Howard, asked to have the executioner's block brought to her cell so she could practice placing her pretty head gracefully upon it, (the knife flicked out) and it was there that an ax chopped through her neck, severing windpipe and spinal cord (the knife flicked shut). It was in the Tower that the sons of Edward IV, children of nine and twelve, were imprisoned by their uncle Richard (the knife flicked out), and it was there that they were smothered in their beds in the middle of the night (the knife flicked shut). It was an awful place, the scene of centuries of violence and bloodshed.

171

"Lady Nithsdale looked at the ancient fortress with its high, gray, crenellated walls, and she was not intimidated. She thought to herself, 'I'm going to break him out.'

"Despite its thick walls, escapes from the Tower were not unheard of. The Tower had not been built as a prison after all, but as a fortress, and even a habitation for the royal family. It wasn't designed, on a fundamental level, to keep people in, but to keep them out.

"Lady Nithsdale noticed this as she went to visit her husband to give him the news that her plea for clemency had been rejected. The earl took the news stoically, as an earl should, and he began writing the speech that he would give on the scaffold. It would be a stirring paean to patriotism, and a reaffirmation of the claim of James III to the British throne. While the earl made plans to die like a man, Lady Nithsdale plotted his escape.

The night before his execution Lady Nithsdale came to visit him with three of her friends. All of them were dressed in long black hooded cloaks, as if in mourning already. They filed into the cell together to commiserate with the doomed man. The earl's cell was connected to a sort of common room where the guards would hang out. Lady Nithsdale thanked these men for treating her husband with humanity and rewarded them with some bottles of French wine. They were grateful, and only too happy to drink to Lord Nithsdale's health.

Once in the cell with her husband she shaved him as close as possible, leaving his face smooth. She then plastered him with makeup, roughed his cheeks, and reddened his lips. One of Lady Nithsdale's friends took off her dress, she was wearing two, and Nithsdale put it on. There was also an extra cloak, which he also put on. They had also brought him a pair of ladies shoes. A few minutes later he walked out of the cell with his wife's friends. The guards, busy drinking and chatting as they were, didn't take notice of the four women leaving through the dim glow of candlelight. Lord Nithsdale walked right out of the Tower of London.

His wife stayed behind, pretending to be in conversation with him. She carried on both halves of their discourse, "Oh my dear, I can't believe I shall have my head chopped off on the morrow," "Do not worry, for you have died in the Lord's cause, and will surely see him in Paradise." After an hour of this she asked the guard to let her out. As she was leaving, she stopped a servant who was about to go into the cell to give the earl more candles. The quick-witted woman asked him not to go in, explaining that her husband had fallen asleep and shouldn't be disturbed.

"With the connivance of the ambassador from Venice, Lord Nithsdale snuck out of the country dressed as a servant, and he and his wife lived long happy lives in France and Italy together."

His story was done and he rewarded himself with another cigarette. "There's one thing that I forgot to mention."

"Oh, what's that?"

"In my novel, they will be robots, all of them. Lord and Lady Nithesby, King George I, James, Anne Boleyn, The Princes in the Tower, the Venetian ambassador. All of them robots."

He tossed the remainder of his cigarette on the ground and walked away.

Chapter 28

I have never been particularly susceptible to loneliness, and when I used to hear people talk about being homesick, I always thought that they were just making it up in an attempt to make those left at home feel better. I've never minded going to a movie by myself, eating a meal by myself, travelling by myself, or just sitting alone in my apartment reading a book and watching television all evening without seeing another human being. I have always been comfortable in my own company.

Living on the streets, I was more surrounded by people than I had ever been. I watched them parade past. So close I could reach out and touch one of them, any of them. There was always somebody nearby, and never a wall between us. And yet I was lonely. For the first time I was lonely. And not only that, I was homesick. I daydreamed about being someplace comfortable and quiet with Abby. Just the two of us. That was my home and it didn't even exist. How could I miss something that had never existed?

It was drizzling and I was sitting in the doorway of a condemned apartment building on Eddy. I read my book and occasionally looked up to watch people pass by. I was reading *A Farewell to Arms* and not liking it nearly as much as I remembered liking it when I read it in college, but I'm not sure I can blame the book. My mind was repeatedly pulled away from the page, not by any specific distraction in the street in front of me, but by sheer weight of loneliness. I looked at the faces of the people who walked by. They were all set. Their necks stiff and locked into a forward position. When the occasional pedestrian glanced in my direction and caught me looking at him, he would quickly look away, determined not to unlock the neck again.

174

I would look away as well, glancing down at my feet and prickling with a vague sense of shame.

In the early afternoon I noticed that I had begun speaking out loud to myself. At first it was just pieces of my interior monologue that seemed to leak from my brain and then drain out of my mouth. They were simple little comments like, "Sure is wet today," "Why do I do such stupid things?" and "I wonder what Abigail is doing." I didn't think much of it. There's nothing wrong with talking to yourself. It's perfectly healthy.

But then a second voice joined the first, and the two didn't seem to get along with each other. One voice would make an observation, and the other would argue with him about it. The second voice was willing to bicker, angrily, about anything. If the first voice said, "Did you see that rat peek out of the storm drain?" the second voice would hiss, "That wasn't a rat. It was just a mouse. Why don't you pay attention for once?"

For a while I tried to stay aloof from the voices, allowing them to speak on any subject they chose. But as the second voice got louder and more unreasonably furious with the first, passersby began to cast worried glances in my direction, and I tried to put a muzzle on the second voice. He didn't like it, and I found it was more effective to get the first voice to be quiet so that the second would have nothing to respond to. Both voices soon fell silent, and the only sound that could be heard was the softly percussive patter of the rain and the hiss of rubber wheels passing on the wet road.

Before today whenever I saw some homeless man talking to himself I always assumed that it was just a symptom of whatever mental disease had driven him into the street in the first place. I now realize that perhaps I was wrong. Maybe when you see street people talking to themselves you are not witnessing a cause of homelessness, but an effect. Maybe the homeless we see talking, yelling, and even screaming into the empty air as we hurry past were not that way when they started living on the street. They could have been quiet and introspective people whose first months or even years of transient living had passed in silence. Then, only when they could take the silence no longer, they found a person to talk to in themselves. The sound of their own voice soothed them, argued with them, or screamed at them. Whatever else it did, it provided them with the fleeting illusion that they were not alone.

I wondered about these voices in my head. Where had they come from? Had they always been there? I comforted myself with the thought that if I had two voices in my head, I would probably be able to find a way to write dialogue when I needed to. I still dreaded the thought of writing that novel. I had been taking notes but had yet to write a single page of the novel itself. One of the things that kept me in the streets for so long was the knowledge that when I went home I would actually have to start grinding out chapters.

Abigail occupied my thoughts more than any other subject. I'm doing this for her. She may never know it, but I'm out here for her. It's a stupid thing I'm doing, but love is a stupid thing itself. Irrational. Foolish. Reckless. And I've always been a rational person. Calculating. Careful. But here I sit, watching the rain, trying to dream up a book so I can write it for a woman. Stupid. Stupid.

In the afternoon, my thoughts were interrupted by a woman who barged into my nest. Her body was cylindrical in shape, she had a red face, and she was wearing an enormous cream-colored cashmere scarf. The combination of these factors made me think of a cupcake with a pile of

176

vanilla frosting and a cherry on top. She had stepped out of the rain holding a bright yellow umbrella and she snapped it shut as she said, "Hello."

"Hi."

"I hope I'm not disturbing you, but I have something important, something life changing, something absolutely fantastic that I would like to discuss with you if have a moment."

She opened the flap of her black leather courier bag as she spoke, and I noticed that it was crammed with pamphlets. I concluded that I had been cornered by some kind of religious zealot, and there would be no escape for me unless I wanted to run out into the rain. The bad news was that I was going to have to sit there and listen to the good news.

"Okay."

"Since prehistoric times," she began in a tone pregnant with drama, "man has turned to one source for solace."

"Mmm."

"To one source for uplift. For a release from burdens and a lightening of the heart."

"Sure."

"Man has repeatedly dipped his head to this spring and drunk deeply from the waters of inspiration and wisdom."

"Yeah."

"But in recent times mankind has turned away and has refused to listen. Mankind has become too hard hearted, too stiff necked, too distracted by the whizz and bang of modern life to pay attention."

"That's too bad."

"Here," she said, as she thrust one of her pamphlets in my direction.

I took it reluctantly.

She continued, "I am spreading the word about poetry."

I looked down at the pamphlet in my hands; the title was, *Collected Poems of Meadowlark Jenson.* "Oh, no," I thought, "I'm dealing with something worse than a religious zealot; I'm dealing with a poet."

"Do you read much poetry?" she asked.

"Uh. A bit."

"What was the last poem you read?"

"I don't know. Something by Robert Frost, probably."

"If people read poets it's always the old ones. Poetry didn't stop when Robert Frost died, you know."

"I know. I think I read some Philip Larkin a while ago."

"Philip Larkin has been dead for something like forty years! You hold Philip Larkin up to me like he is some fresh rose you have just plucked for the sniffing! There are fresher flowers!"

"Such as," I looked down at the pamphlet, "Meadowlark Jenson?"

"Yes, exactly like Meadowlark Jenson."

"Didn't he used to play for the Harlem Globetrotters?"

"No. That's a different Meadowlark. Meadowlark Lemon. When I chose my *nom de plume* I hadn't ever heard of him. I wish people would stop throwing him in my face."

"I'm sorry."

"That's quite alright; I'm used to it by now."

"You know, I actually like poetry."

"Oh sure, everybody says they like poetry, but nobody reads it. Even reading novels has become too hard for most people. Nobody reads anymore. Surfing the internet isn't reading, it's just letting words and images wash over you. You spend all your time surfing the internet, I suppose? Poking people on Facebook, twittering them, sending them Instagrams?"

"I don't have the internet."

"The lack of social media is the one big advantage the homeless have over the rest of us."

She was right about that, and I told her so.

"I'll let you get to reading," she gestured towards the pamphlet she had given me, "and the rain won't stop me from spreading the good word." With that she popped her umbrella open and headed back into the drizzle, leaving me with a slightly damp copy of her collected works wilting in my hands. I read all the poems in her pamphlet (it only took a half hour) and they were about what you would expect, except for the very last one which spoke to me somehow.

My skill as a writer has won me
An audience of one (me).
And she's a cheap one too
Always searching Amazon
For the daily deal and
Never paying dollars when
Dimes will do. Skimming
Remainder bins, binging
At used bookstores.
She's a redoubtable rereader.
And she's read my books
Many, many times.
Though each time
With a presumptuously red pencil.

Chapter 29

The efforts to rebrand one of the most benighted bits of the Tenderloin as "Little Saigon" in a sad attempt to trick tourists into visiting that terrifying neighborhood, had largely failed, but a small Vietnamese community did actually live there. One or two shops specializing in goods from their homeland existed, and there were also a half dozen Vietnamese restaurants in the area. I was eating, not at one of these restaurants, but at a small liquor store where an ancient Vietnamese couple sold banh mi sandwiches with meat cooked in two big crock pots crusted with layers of baked on grease that they kept behind the counter. They brightened the heavy flavor of the pork with shredded carrots, cilantro, and thick slices of jalapeno peppers. All these ingredients were wedged into sections of baguette *bien cuit*, and the resulting taste was like a French kiss from a pagan goddess. And the price? $2.50 per sandwich. Being poor was terrible, but sandwiches like those soothed the sting.

I was in a pretty good mood as I stepped out of the store, biting into my second sandwich with a burst of crumbs and spicy sauce. I had a paperback copy of Joseph Conrad's novel *Victory* in my back pocket, and I intended to find a quiet spot where I could read it. I had picked *Victory* up at a used bookstore the day before. I remember reading somewhere that Joan Didion always turned to that book for inspiration before beginning to write another novel of her own, and if it's good enough to inspire Joan Didion, maybe it would inspire me. I had already read the first chapter and I was into it. It was looking like it would be a good day to be homeless. My plan was to mix reading with panhandling, with reading first. I walked a few blocks to the Civic Center, sat on the stairs of City Hall, and began to read.

I had only read a few pages when, for reasons I could not define, I began to feel uncomfortable. It wasn't a physical discomfort, although the stairs were both cold and hard; it was a spiritual discomfort. A mental unease. And it wasn't the book that was causing this feeling, although Conrad can certainly be dark when he wants to be, and his characters chronically suffer from unease. But this was something more than that. I sensed an evil sort of presence. I felt something dark and malevolent nearby, and when I looked up, there was Proctor with his bald head gleaming in the sun like an alabaster dome in the center of a sinful city.

He was smiling at me, "You really seem to be into your book there." Here was another man who didn't respect book walls.

"What do you want, Proctor?"

"Whoa! Why the tone? We're friends here, aren't we? Let's keep things amicable!"

I didn't respond.

"You like that word, by the way, 'amicable'? I read that on my word of the day calendar this morning and I knew right away when and how I was gonna use it. You gotta use these new words or you forget them. So I always try to use them on the same day when I first see them and this morning I knew it was going to be easy. It isn't always easy, by the way. Last Friday the word of the day was 'haberdasher' and I gotta admit that I could not find a way to jam it into a conversation. I think the guys at O'Bannon's would have laughed at me if I'd thrown it at them. You ever use that word, 'haberdasher'?"

"Not often, no."

"Really? Smart, educated guy like you? I'd think you'd be haberdashing all over the place."

"What do you want from me?"

181

"Want something? Me? Nothing. I' just here to catch up with an old acquaintance. Can't a guy say 'hi' without everybody accusing him of wanting something? We shared our stories, and in my book, that means that we are more than acquaintances now. We're friends."

"I never told you my story."

"You didn't need to. I know all about it. It's about that girl I saw you eating lunch with, Abigail Park. Did you even know her last name? You could use her name in the title of your book, something like *I, Abigail*. Sometimes just a name can be a good title, like *Lolita* or *Bunnicula*. I gotta say she's a very interesting character. I'd hate to see a good character like that wasted on a book with a sad ending."

We were both silent for a moment.

"Remember. Saturday. It's going to cost you $1,000 to keep your book from being a tearjerker."

I had begun to think that I'd simply never see Proctor again. After all, he hadn't known much about me, and I'd hoped that he knew nothing about Abby, but apparently he had found some things out. That had been the purpose of this little conversation, he was letting me know that he knew how to find me, and how to find Abby, and reminding me that he wanted to be paid.

The problem wasn't that I didn't have $1,000 to give him. I did. But everyone knows that once a blackmailer starts to squeeze you, he never stops. And since my plan was to be with Abby for the rest of my life, that's how long the squeezing would continue. The right thing to do would be to confess everything to Abby. But how could I do that? I know that it's a bad idea to start a relationship with somebody while you are keeping a secret from them, but the relationship would never start at all if I told her that I had tried to hire a private detective to track her down.

182

Chapter 18

I was sitting in one of the dingier and more fish scented corners of Chinatown, reading a paperback Bernie Gunther novel and sipping on a glass of Coke, when the man at the next table struck up a conversation with me. Normally I would have tried to shut him out. At that moment, however, I was ready to talk with someone. I may be a solitary man by instinct, but it's getting to be too much; everyone treats me like a noseless leper. I was greedy for whatever scraps of conversation I could get.

"Do you mind if I sit next to you?" the stranger asked.

"No, go right ahead." I gave the man a once over with my right eyeball, hoping that his appearance would somehow betray his intentions. People don't go out of their way to speak with the homeless, so I was a bit suspicious. He was wearing a black Giants baseball cap with orange lettering. This cap was pushed down upon a mop of curly brown hair that poofed up anywhere it was not contained by the hat. He had a five-day beard that was lightly salted with gray hairs, but despite the gray he appeared to be in his early thirties. He was wearing faded jeans, worn work boots, and a red fleece jacket. A gold Rolex was strapped around his wrist.

"Am I right in assuming you're homeless?"

"Yeah"

"I suppose you're hard up for money?"

"Yeah. That's sort of part of the deal when you're homeless."

He smiled, "Sure, but you could always be one of those crazy bums they find dead on the street with wads of cash stuffed into a garbage bag."

"I don't even have a garbage bag."

He laughed. It was a patronizing sort of laugh. I decided that his conversation wasn't worth it and got to the point, "What do you want?"

"I want to offer you a job."

"What do you pay?"

"I'll give you fifty bucks. And a bit of meth."

The thought of earning fifty dollars made me a little giddy. "I don't want any meth, but what do I have to do to earn the fifty dollars?"

"I'm a movie producer, and I'm looking for some homeless people to help out as . . . extras."

"Extras?"

"Well, no, not extras really. . . more like stuntmen."

"I don't know anything about doing stunts."

"You don't need to. That's the beauty of it. All you need is the courage to try. That's why I'd like to give you a little shot of something first, it really boosts the courage."

"Dutch courage is one thing; Bakersfield courage is too much. And drugs don't boost courage; they impair judgment."

He laughed again, with that awful laugh that attempted to ingratiate but grated instead, "Same thing." My toes had been feeling much better, but something about being next to this guy make them itchy again.

"What kind of movie is this going to be anyway?"

"It's called 'Homeless Highlight Reel'."

"Is it like those Bumfight movies those kids in San Diego were making years ago?"

"Kind of."

"Didn't they go to jail?"

"I don't think so. Besides, we've had our lawyers go over the project and we're sure that we're bulletproof. Will you do it?"

"I'm not going to fight anyone."

"You won't have to. We have a cool stunt all lined up for you. Just come and check it out. If you don't like the look of it, you don't have to do it."

"All right," I said as I remembered my vow to go out and gain some life experiences.

At that moment, a black child-abductor kind of van pulled up outside the cafe. "Good, here's my crew." I would never have gotten into the van except that there was a voice in my head saying, "She will never love an unpublished man, and you need experience to have something to write about."

The van smelled like a wet dog. There were only two seats, one for the driver and one for the passenger. They didn't let me drive and Gary took the passenger seat, so I sat in the back. It was dark in the deep recesses of the van because the glass in all the back windows had been painted over black. I sat on a large trunk and tried not to slide too much while empty bottles of Mountain Dew and Budweiser rolled around my ankles. A shopping cart had been overturned in the van's nether reaches.

Gary's crew consisted of one man. His name was Willie, and he looked like he was just a half step above living in the street himself. He had a long gray beard that forked at the end and a silver mullet that was slicked back with his natural grease. He was wearing a denim shirt, denim pants, and a denim vest. Willie's voice was gravelly when he spoke to Gary: "So what does this guy want?"

"Nothing, he says he's going to do it clean."

Willie thought about this for a moment and then said, "I doubt it."

"By the way, how's Gerardo? Did you get his finger reattached?"

"Naw, we couldn't find it."

"Oh."

"He didn't need it anyway. He's still got eight other fingers he can scratch himself with."

They had been speaking to each other as if I wasn't there, and I decided to intrude upon their private conversation.

"Who's Gerardo?"

"Just a guy we know."

"Where are we going?"

"The Lyon Street stairs."

San Francisco is a city famous for its hills. There are many of them, and many of them are very steep. To the people driving them some of the streets seem to be nearly vertical. As you approach intersections on such streets the blacktop disappears and you experience the illusion that your car has left the earth and is bound for the skies. There are some places, however, where it is simply too steep to build a road. In such areas there are staircases instead. The Lyon Street stairs are perhaps the most famous of these. Lyon Street gradually climbs from the South up the hill to towards the bay, and then nosedives down the other side. It's like a roller coaster: clank, clank, clank, you go slowly up a modest incline, and then *whoosh* when you hit the other side. There's just a bit more road and then, boom, some very steep stairs.

The stairs on that incline are bordered with beautifully manicured bushes and colorful flowers. As you descend them you can enjoy the sight of glitzy mansions on your right, tall eucalyptus trees from the Presidio on your left, and the San Francisco bay immediately in front of you. Millionaires live all over San Francisco, but this little corner is for billionaires. As I stood atop Lyon Street this time, however, I noticed nothing but the concrete stairs themselves. They are steep, they are hard, and Gary wanted me to go down them in a shopping cart.

"But I'll be killed!"

"You won't be killed. Look, we even have a helmet for you." Gary pulled out a yellow kayaking helmet with the Hobo Highlights Logo painted on it.

I glanced back down the stairs. If my life had been a comic movie from the 80s starring Chevy Chase, I knew exactly what would happen if I went down those stairs in that cart. I saw it all flash before my mind's eye. I would get in the cart, shakily, with fear in my every movement. I would then have second thoughts. As I started to climb back out of the cart Willie would give it a nudge and I would yell "whooooooah" as the it started its descent. I would be shaken violently by the stairs and would comically shout, "I-I-I-I-I th-th-th-think m-m-m-m-my fillllllings a-a-a-re sh-sh-shaking loose!" I would break through banisters and plough through bushes until my cart was launched off the end of the stairs and started down the rest of Lyon Street. I would have wood splinters and leaves in my hair at this point.

As I picked up speed my shopping cart would careen into the tables of a sidewalk café. I would knock over a table occupied by two gay men. They would be unruffled, and one would say with a swishy lisp, "That train sure had a nice caboose." The audience would groan at this, and later LGBTQ groups would hold press conferences to complain about it. As I crossed Lombard I would almost be hit by a bus, but the bus would swerve to miss me and would crash into a fruit stand instead. Never mind that normally Lombard street is as fruitstandless as the moon. I would then speed through a wedding at the Palace of Fine Arts, where I would smash into the wedding cake and hit an attractive bridesmaid. She would flip up into the air and land, unharmed, in my cart (probably in some sort of

188

sexually suggestive position). We would both be covered with frosting from the cake. My ride wouldn't stop until my cart blasted off the end of a pier and landed in a garbage barge.

But my life was not a Chevy Chase comedy from the 80s. It was looking more and more like a gritty tragedy from the 70s, and as such my ride was sure to be less entertaining, and far more likely to result in permanent injury. I would probably navigate no more than a half dozen stairs before the top-heavy cart tipped over and I spilled out onto the concrete. It would hurt, and it would be humiliating in indefinable ways.

But again, maybe this would be an experience I could use in my novel somehow. I took the helmet from Gary's outstretched hand and fastened it to my head with the chin strap. Willie held the cart steady as I boarded it.

I hadn't sat in a shopping cart since I was about four years old and I didn't remember them being so high off the ground. Now that I was in there it shocked me that any parent would let their child ride around at such an altitude. And the cart seemed to have been designed with an eye to making it as rickety as possible while leaving out all other considerations. Gary had skipped to the bottom of the first flight of stairs and was standing with the camera pointed upward. He yelled some last-minute advice: "Try to crash *before* you get to me!"

"When do I get my money?"

"As soon as you do the stunt!"

"Can I get half now?"

"No! Now come on! It'll be great! You're going to be a movie star!"

At that moment I realized I had made a mistake. This wasn't worth it. This was stupid. Nope. I wasn't going to do it. I started to get up, but Willie nudged the cart and it

189

started to rattle down the steps. At that moment I didn't feel angry at Gary and Willie for putting me in peril. There was no room for anger. My mind only had space for fear. I leaned back as far as I could in an attempt to prevent a faceplant. Falling to the back or to the side, and the sooner the better, was the best policy. But I had no control, the cart was going to do whatever it wanted and I had no more to say about its direction than a flea riding on a bear. After about ten steps the cart slammed into the railing, swung sideways and rolled.

Or, at least, that's what I think happened. I passed out at about the fifth step. Apparently when your mind is overwhelmed by fear it shuts itself off. I don't think I was out for too long, but when I awoke Willie and Gary were gone and they had taken my helmet with them. They had also taken the money they promised. The shopping cart was still there. It was resting on top of me. I was sore everywhere, but had apparently only suffered bruising. I picked myself up and ascended the stairs with a limping gait. Gary had at least been kind enough to toss my backpack out of his van before speeding away from the crime scene. I hoisted it to my shoulders and hobbled away in search of a place to sleep.

Chapter 31

"I shouldn't be here," she said.

The woman sitting across the table wasn't looking at me when she spoke. Her voice was so soft that it was almost entirely absorbed in the hubbub of the crowded cafeteria. She had her face pointed downward at her meal of green beans, fried chicken, and mashed potatoes, and for a moment I didn't even realize that she had been speaking to me.

"Excuse me?" I said.

"I shouldn't be here."

"Me either."

"I mean it. This place is for poor people, and I have, not money exactly, but I have property. Valuable property."

She clearly wanted to tell me about it but needed just a little prodding before she could, so I prodded. "Really? What brings you here then?"

"I can't convert my property into cash. It's valuable, but I'm having a hard time selling it."

"What is it? If you don't mind telling me."

"I don't mind. I'll show you."

I studied her face for a moment as she turned to unzip the backpack hanging sideways from her chair. She was young, early to mid-twenties, and looked soft and relatively unmarked by whatever life had brought her to eat in a cafeteria run by a charity. Curly blond hair spilled out of her beanie and partially obstructed her green eyes that were veined red but unmarked by lines. I was not surprised when she pulled a manuscript from her backpack and pushed it across the table to me. I read the title, *The Vampiriad*.

"I see what you mean," I told her, "manuscripts aren't very liquid."

"No."

"What's it about?"

She told me. It was a YA science fiction story about an arc ship flying through deep space when one of the cryopods opens and releases its passenger, a vampire. His plan is to spend the next 200 years sucking the ship's other occupants dry when he notices a beautiful girl in one of the pods. Instead of sucking her blood, he wakes her and together they use science to synthesize blood out of vegetables so he doesn't have to kill anymore. Then the two of them have to fight a group of hostile aliens who teleport onto their ship, forcing the vampire not only to kill again, but to turn his girlfriend into a vampire to keep her safe.

It sounded pretty good to me, and I told her so.

"I think so too. I hope so. I worked on it for 1,332 hours."

"You counted?"

"I approximated. I added it all up when I was done."

"That's impressive."

She didn't reply.

"Can't get it published?"

"No."

"I'm sorry."

"Did you know that if I had spent all that time working at a job that paid me $23 per hour I would have earned $33,000 dollars?"

"Why $23?"

"That's what I was getting paid in my regular job when I started writing it."

"Oh."

"Publishing is a pyramid scheme."

I chuckled but it was cut short when I saw how deadly serious she was. "What do you mean?"

"I feel like I was scammed. People say that buying lottery tickets is a scam. They say that it is a tax on stupidity. But if I buy a lottery ticket, how much money have I lost?"

"I don't know. I've never bought a lottery ticket."

"A few dollars. That's all. Just a few dollars to get into the game. I spent two years putting together a lottery ticket that cost me $33,000." She took her book back from me and looked at it mournfully. "Why didn't anybody tell me that I was just paying a tax on my false hope?" Anger flashed red across her face and for a moment I thought she might throw the book as hard as she could or to tear it apart like a freak with a phonebook at a strongman competition. Instead the red drained back to white and she put the book away in her backpack again.

"Maybe you just haven't put it into the right hands yet. Maybe it needs a little more work?"

"No. I've put it into every hand I could find, and they have all just thrown it back at me. Nobody wants it. Nobody will ever want it." I almost repeated the sacred litany beginning with *Carrie*'s 30 rejections and ending with *Harry Potter*'s twelve, but I could tell that it wouldn't work. She had lost her faith.

I tried a different approach, "But, and I say this without ever having written anything, but isn't artistic creation its own reward?"

"Yes. In some ways, I guess. I still love my stupid book, whether anyone else does or not. A work of art is your baby, even if it's nothing but science fiction aimed at teenage girls. I've spent the past year watching people spit on my baby. I don't love my baby any less, but it hurts to know nobody loves it but me."

Chapter 32

I woke up on Saturday morning with no intention of visiting Proctor in his shabby office on Turk Street. Wise men will tell you that you can't just ignore your problems and hope that they will go away, and I suppose the wise men are generally right, but since when do people do the right thing? It's so easy to put off an unpleasant bit of business, and that's what I had decided to do.

I spent the day wandering around. Maybe I had some instinct, a holdover from our hunter-gatherer days, telling me that Proctor wouldn't be able to find a moving target. It was a fine day, sunny and cool but not cold and the breeze was so light that it was only slightly annoying.

In the early evening I walked to the Safeway in the Marina and bought a baguette and some cheese and then crossed the street and sat on a bench that was pointed towards the bay. I watched the usual parade of pleasure boats, tourist ferries, and container ships as I ate my bread and cheese and washed it down with a beer. I felt good. I felt relaxed. A simple meal, a sunny day, and a beautiful view… who needed a home when there were moments like this one to be lived outside?

Then somebody moved into the edge of my peripheral vision and sat down on the other end of the bench. When I glanced over, my heart sank. It was Proctor. He was my problem. I had ignored him, and he had not just gone away. The wise men had been right again.

"You know what the word of the day was today?"

"I guess you're going to tell me."

"What kinda guy would I be if I self-improved myself by growing my vocabulary without taking the time to share what I learned?"

I didn't answer.

194

"I'd be a real heel, that's what. Well, today's word was 'schadenfreude.' You know what that means?"

"Yes."

"I knew you were a smart guy. Well, it was a new one for me. You gotta hand it to the Germans, coming up with a word like that. I'll bet you think that I'm the kinda guy who really gets into this schadenfreude stuff, but that's not the case. Making people unhappy doesn't do anything for me, but I do gotta get paid."

"I'm not paying you anything. Go away."

"I know we didn't settle on a specific hour for our meeting, but the more I thought about it, the more I thought, 'You know what? I don't think that guy is gonna come. I don't think he's gonna do the decent thing and keep his engagement. He's probably gonna get a big case of schadenfreude just thinking about me sitting around in my office all day. All lonely. Waiting for him to show up as the sun sets.' Was I wrong?"

"What engagement? There's no engagement if one person says, 'come over' and the other person never agrees that he will."

"Fair enough. You make a point. Still, it would have been nice if you had come over. It would have been polite. It would have saved me trouble, and if you make trouble for me, well, that's just making trouble for yourself, really. And who needs it?"

"How did you find me?"

"Ahh, well, I'm not going to tell you that. It would spoil the fun. A magician isn't supposed to give up his tricks, remember? All you need to know is that I can find you whenever I want. That was the skill that you were going to hire me for, and now you know that I'm good at it. You can't avoid me. You can put me next to death and taxes on

195

the list of things you'll never get away from. And Abigail Park can't avoid me either, unless you do the right thing."

He scooted closer to me and his bulk caused such a dip in the middle of the bench that I could feel myself almost sliding in his direction. He smelled of garlic and peppermint. "So, do you have the thousand bucks I asked for?"

"Do I look like I have a thousand dollars?"

"No, you don't. That's one of the things I can't figure about you. You don't look like you have any money, but you gotta have some. How were you going to pay me when you were trying to hire me?"

"Maybe I was going to stiff you."

"No, that's not it." As he said this another person sat down on the far end of the bench and both of us looked over to see who it was. It was the Knifeman. He didn't talk to us, but he put a fresh cigarette in his mouth and lit it. When he took a pull the tip of his cigarette twinkled in the deepening night with the impersonal light of a distant star. Then he pulled his knife out and began to flick it open and shut, open and shut. Proctor watched this action nervously for a full minute, studying the man, before deciding that the knife wasn't a threat. It was just the tic of a man who wasn't quite right in the head.

Proctor continued talking to me, "Let me tell you my story," he said.

"I've heard it before."

"Of course you don't want to hear it again, but you need to. I've improved it. Killed some of my darlings. So, I'm going to tell it to you, and you're going to sit there and listen, or else there will be consequences."

I sat there and listened.

"It's about this guy, a little weasel who owes money to a private detective. This detective, he doesn't like deadbeats,

196

he doesn't like people who don't pay up when they should. So he noses around a little. Finds out about this guy, what his name is, where he works. He finds out that he makes a good living, that he has a nice place in Pacific Heights. So when this weasel tries to pretend he's a bum and says he doesn't have any money, well, the private dick knows better. And since he doesn't like being lied to, he tells the guy that it's no longer $1,000 that he owes, it's $2,000, and it's gonna keep going up if he doesn't act right."

"This is blackmail!" I shouted. "Did you hear that?" I asked the Knifeman, "This guy is trying to blackmail me!"

"Who said anything about blackmail?"

"I did! And this time there's a witness!" But when I looked over at the Knifeman, he was completely zoned out. He was paying no attention to us; he just sat there, unperturbed by our dispute, smoking and flicking that knife.

"Who's a witness?" Proctor said with a chuckle, "That guy? He's not the type to witness anything. Besides, we're just telling stories, aren't we? It was the plot of the novel I'm working on. You shouldn't take it literally. It's way out there. In fact, it's a science fiction story, everybody in it is a robot. The detective, the weasel, the hot Asian girl. All of them are robots."

The Knifeman froze when he heard this. The blade was locked in its open position. He was no longer puffing on his cigarette; it sat in his still lips and smoldered dully. Proctor hadn't seen any of this, but I had. The Knifeman spoke, "What did you say?"

Proctor turned to look at him, "It's not any of your business, but I said that it's not a real story, everybody in it is a robot."

"A robot?"

"Yeah. Listen, buddy, I'm talking to this guy over here, please don't butt in on something that's got nothing to do with you."

"Where did you get the idea to have everyone be a robot?"

"It just came to me."

"Just came to you?"

"That's right, now will you go away?"

"You stole it."

"I didn't steal anything, and this has nothin' to do with you."

"You stole it," there was a menace in the Knifeman's voice now.

Proctor stared at him, glanced at the knife, and realized that he was in danger. "Look, I think there has been a…"

"You stole it."

"... misunderstanding here. I didn't mean to take any…"

"YOU STOLE IT!"

"... body's idea. You know what, in fact, I misspoke, they aren't... "

"YOU STOLE IT!"

"... robots at all, they're space aliens and …"

The cigarette dropped from the Knifeman's lips as the knife in his hand plunged into Proctor's chest. The blade flashed in and out like the needle on a sewing machine. It punctured Proctor's chest six or seven times before I could even process what was happening. A man was being murdered right in front of me. Each stab was going right to the knife's handle, and I was certain that its steel was touching vital organs with every stroke.

Finally, I gathered my wits enough to shout "STOP! STOP!" and I even made an instinctive motion to push the Knifeman away from Proctor, but it was already over. The Knifeman stood and fled across the grass as people who had been doing yoga or walking their dogs in the last fleeting rags of the sunset ran up to assist Proctor. I was trying to put pressure on his wounds with my bare hands, but nothing was to be done. He was a dead man.

I had ignored the problem, and it had gone away in spectacular fashion.

Chapter 33

When I read mystery novels I am constantly annoyed by witnesses who don't cough up all the relevant evidence in a timely fashion. They always have this or that bogus little excuse for keeping vital information back from the police, but, really, the reader knows that the only reason the witness is keeping his mouth shut is because if the witness told all he knew when first questioned, the mystery novel would come to an abrupt end. The novelist has to be parsimonious in his parceling out of clues.

But this isn't a mystery novel, and when I failed to disclose certain details to the police yesterday it wasn't out of any attempt to ramp up the drama. I kept back a smidge of information because it wouldn't have looked good for me. You and I both know that I didn't murder Proctor. But even though the Knifeman was clearly the murderer, and there were witnesses who saw him running away with a knife in his hand (though apparently none who saw him actually sticking it into Proctor's body), if I told the police that I had almost hired him to find a woman for me, that he had blackmailed me, and that at the time he was murdered he was reiterating his blackmail threats... well, it wouldn't have looked good. The police might have assumed that I had hired the Knifeman to kill the detective. I had warned Proctor that blackmailers always get murdered in mystery novels, and it's almost always one of the blackmail victims who does it. The police know this fact as well as I do. If I had been entirely open about my relationship with Proctor, I would have become a suspect.

I kept the blackmail off the radar. I told the police that the murder victim, a stranger, had sat down next to me to tell me the plot of his novel and that when he revealed his twist ending, the Knifeman, who had been clicking his knife open and shut while I talked to Proctor, became agitated, accused him of stealing his story idea, and then stabbed him multiple times before running away.

"What was the twist?" The cop asked. He was a grizzled veteran of the old school, radiating toughness and completely devoid of nonsense or tomfoolery of any kind. He was wearing a suit that seemed to have been bought in the 80s and was accessorized with a wide red tie that was clearly a relic from the 70s. He had a look in his eye that seemed to say, with the utmost politeness, "Please provide me with an excuse to give you a thorough beating."

"All the characters in the story, who the reader has been led to believe were human, turn out to be robots."

The cop whistled appreciatively, "That's a real good ending. I might use it myself. I mean, this Proctor guy doesn't need it anymore."

"What's your novel about?" I asked him.

He spent ten minutes relating the plot to his novel. He had yet to write a single page, but it was going to be called "Space Cop: 2355," and it was about an officer in the "space police" who goes around flashing his "space badge," solving "space crime," arresting "space criminals," eating "space donuts," and making space safe for "space folks." Lost in his fictional world he forgot to interrogate me anymore and let me go as soon as he was done telling his story. I glanced at the pad where he had been taking notes; all it said was, "It turns out they are all robots!!!!"

Chapter 34

If you'll think back to Chapter 3 (the most important chapter because it's the one where I met Abby) you'll recall that I told Abby that my book was going to be about homelessness and crime. I had been homeless for almost three weeks, but other than a minor trespass or two, I had committed no crimes. As the end of my project approached, I realized that it was time to move in this new direction.

I decided to become a street hustler, a minor con man. I had been living a lie ever since I left my home, so, in a way I had been a con man all along. In fact, every time I begged a dollar I had been conning the person who gave it to me. I didn't really need it, and I wasn't desperate. I had been nowhere near the end of my rope. I had been playing this little game of falsehood for nickels and dimes, and now I intended to set my sights a little higher.

When I say that I planned to become a con man, I don't want you to get any inflated ideas about the capers I intended to pull. I wasn't going to sell the Brooklyn Bridge or the Eiffel Tower. I wasn't going to build a pyramid scheme to fleece hordes of foolish investors (while also, with the irony of pyramid schemes, making a few foolish investors rich). I would be working no long cons of any kind. I'd be playing the short game. I've been the target of minor acts of trickery in my life and I had learned a few scams that I thought it might be interesting to try.

The last little push into criminality occurred when I found a set of keys in the gutter. The keys were for a Lexus and they reminded me of a classic con that had been attempted on me twice in the last few years. Though in my case it hadn't work, I was convinced that there were people out there who might be more susceptible to it. There may be no documentary proof to the old maxim that there's a sucker

born every minute, but it instinctively feels right, and I
intended to go out there and find some of those suckers.

Doing anything criminal was completely against my
natural instincts. I have always been a law-abiding man.
And before becoming a law-abiding man, I was a law
abiding child. Many people have a story about filching a
candy bar at the grocery store when their mother wasn't
looking. I didn't have one. I had never filched a candy bar.

You may remember that in Chapter 2 I mentioned that I
had been a Boy Scout. Being a Boy Scout isn't,
unfortunately, proof of honesty. When we rolled into a truck
stop on our way to a camping trip, the members of Troop
763 could be counted on to steal all the merchandise they
could fit into their olive green standard issue Boy Scouts of
America cargo shorts. If there had been a merit badge for
shoplifting, half the members of my troop would have
earned it without even trying. I would not have earned it. I
paid full price for my Mountain Dew and my Snickers Bar. I
was the Boy Scout in stereotype, not the Boy Scout in fact.

But I had to do it. Being homeless, it turns out, is mostly
just panhandling and laying around, and I worried that
panhandling and laying around were ingredients that
wouldn't be spicy enough to help me cook a tasty novel. If I
was going to rise above Chadwick Blowington and impress
Abigail, I had to do it. I had to go out there and ill-get some
gains.

My plan required that I purchase a suit. Suits are not
cheap and buying a new one was, of course, out of the
question. Goodwill came to my rescue. After only five
minutes in the thrift store I found a black wool number
hanging on the rack. It fit, or at least came fairly close to
fitting. The arms were a wee bit long and it was also a wee
bit too wide in the waist, but I'd have to just make due since
I couldn't afford to have it altered. By itself the suit cost

203

twenty-five dollars. Black shoes, a belt, a tie and a white shirt added another thirty dollars to my bill. After my spending spree was over I only had about thirty-five dollars left. This is okay, however, because I am not wasting the money; I am investing it. Investing it in myself.

After making my purchases I checked into the O'Farrell Palace Hotel. It was as dumpy as ever. I took a shower, shaved, and put on my suit. I then spent a good half hour admiring the dashing figure I cut in my new outfit. It was a little worn on the seat and at the elbows, but I didn't look like a bum anymore. I looked respectable. I looked like the sort of person who works in a carpeted cubicle beneath soul sucking fluorescent lighting. I looked like a guy with a white-collar job who gets paid much less than the average blue collar laborer despite a four year degree in business with an emphasis in management. I looked like the sort of person who spends most of his time at work playing fantasy sports on the internet and getting paid very little for it. There was no reason on earth why anyone should doubt any story I told them. People in suits, even suits that are just a little bit shabby, and don't fit quite right, are trustworthy. That's the illusion that our entire democratic government is based upon, and I planned to turn it to my advantage.

It is possible that you are asking yourself why I didn't just go home at this point. If I was done being homeless and wasn't going to be sleeping on the street, why not just go sleep in my own bed? But I knew that I couldn't. In some ways I had become a different person in the past weeks. This new me might be able to con some chumps out of their hard-earned dollars. There was no way the old me could do it, and I knew that the moment I walked through the front door of my apartment, the old me would reassert himself and immediately crush the bit of me that was capable of

204

committing a crime. I was getting closer, but I couldn't go home yet.

I stepped out of my room at the O'Farrell Palace Hotel the next morning feeling like a carefree flaneur of the old school. I was wearing my suit proudly as I walked towards Fisherman's Wharf. I had not been back to the Wharf since my first day on the street when I so conspicuously failed in my first attempt at panhandling. I had no worries that I would fail in my new pursuit. I had learned a lot about myself and gained a great deal of confidence in the past couple of weeks, and I was certain that I would succeed. The waterfront would be teeming with tourists with a lot of disposable cash but little disposable intelligence. It would be a place ripe for felonious picking.

I stopped at a small diner and ate breakfast while reading the morning paper. (It was a paper that I had purchased with my own change, not one I had scavenged from a recently deserted table.) I took my time and read the comics and the *Datebook*. I checked the box scores and skimmed a human-interest story about a recent immigrant from Cambodia who had opened a taco stand in the Mission. It didn't feel like a morning to be reading serious news. The day was to be one of happiness and triumph. I saw myself as a smaller scale version of Paul Newman's character in *The Sting*.

When I arrived at the wharf it was ten in the morning and tourists were already walking the streets. I ditched my backpack in a broken newspaper vending machine and went in search of a mark. I wanted a tourist who didn't look like he was from a big city, someone who had the small town "aw shucks" Christian personality stamped on their very soul. I wanted an honest person who projected his honesty on the world at large. I wanted someone who was clearly of a giving disposition. I wanted an innocent, the proverbial babe in the woods.

205

After a while I spotted a woman on a bench near Pier 39. She was alone, which was good. I didn't want the mark to be with anyone who might talk them out of giving me money, and few people come to tourist traps like Fisherman's Wharf alone. She was rather plain looking and appeared to be in her mid-thirties. She was wide eyed and clearly enjoying all the sights and sounds that the City had to offer. I approached her confidently.

"Hello," I said.

She looked at me for a moment before responding.

"Hi."

"I'm sorry to disturb you but I'm in a bit of a predicament."

"Oh, I sorry, what's wrong?"   She sized me up, and the magical conservative suit appeared to convince her that I posed no threat, even to a bumpkin like her.

"Well . . . this is embarrassing . . . I hate asking for help." I hadn't acted since being cast as a pirate in my High School's production of "The Pirates of Penzance" but I was playing my part well now. The rust had quickly fallen from my acting skills.

"Oh no, that's okay, I'd be glad to help if I can." She had already given a tenuous agreement before I'd even told her what was desired. At this early stage things were going even better than I had anticipated.

"Well, you see . . ." I paused to highlight how painfully embarrassing this all was before proceeding, "I'm not from San Francisco . . ."

"Me either."

"Really?" I had built some common ground between us, we were both strangers in a strange land and had to rely on one another, "Well, I, uh, I'm from Reno. I'm an associate at a small law firm there, and I came here on business for one of our clients. I parked my car somewhere, apparently illegally, and the city towed it."

"Oh, that's terrible!"

"I know, and it is going to cost $215 to get it out. The problem is that I was pickpocketed while riding the bus - watch out for the busses, they're full of thieves - on my way to get my car out. I lost all my cash and my credit cards."

"Oh dear."

"At least I still have my keys," I flashed the Lexus keys to punctuate the declaration and to provide my story with a piece of physical evidence. Minor con men don't drive luxury cars! The keys, like the suit, were a badge of my honesty. *People who already have enough money to buy an expensive car don't have to hustle just to get a few dollars more. He's telling the truth.*

"That's terrible!"

"It's been such an ordeal. I've been trying to get a hold of my wife, but she's not answering the phone and I just can't find a way to scrape the money together."

"I'm so sorry, what can I do to help?" She was earnestly concerned with my predicament, and there was not a hint of doubt in her voice. I was going to score; I just knew it.

"Well, I need a couple hundred dollars to get the car out, and, if you could just loan me part of it, I would really appreciate it. I'll pay you right back. I'll have the money in the mail before you get back to wherever you are from . . . I feel so stupid asking you . . . I'm really sorry to put you on the spot like this." I said this, the Boy Scout inside me reasserted himself, informing me sternly "You really are going to give this woman her money back." I realized that I actually would mail any money she gave me right back to her. Fraud sounded fun, but now that I was committing it, I realized it just wasn't for me.

"Don't be silly, we're all on this earth to help one another," she said as she began rummaging about in her purse.

"Thank you so much."

"All I've got on me is seventy dollars," she said apologetically, "my husband is off buying tickets for Alcatraz and if you'll just wait a few minutes for him I can probably get you a little more."

"Oh no, I don't want to bother you any more than necessary. Seventy dollars would be terrific. I'm sure I'll find some other Good Samaritan (a biblical reference couldn't hurt) who'll help me with the rest. Thank you so much." A bird in the hand, as they say, is worth two in the bush, and seventy dollars was more than I expected to get out of any one mark anyway. The husband might have caused problems, so I decided to take the offered money and run. She handed me three twenty-dollar bills and two five dollar bills.

"*Thank you so much*" I repeated as I slipped the cash into my pocket. I then pulled out a scrap of paper and a pen. "Now where can I return the money?"

She gave me her address (some small town in Colorado) and I thanked her yet again as we parted. In the space of a few minutes I had taken in seventy dollars. That was as much as I made in an entire day working for Tony. I knew that I had been lucky, and that people with such a perfect combination of soft heart and soft head would be hard to come by, but if I could only find a few of them every day I would do just fine in my new line of work.

As I thought things over, however, I soon realized that my plan to become a con man had been a mistake. If I didn't have the heart to keep the money people gave to me, then what was I doing but borrowing from them? If I kept the money, I was committing fraud, if I didn't then I was borrowing. I wasn't going to keep the money. So, at no point was I actually committing a crime. I was lying to them, true, but without stealing as well, it all felt sort of hallow.

I was standing near the water, thinking these things over, when I was tapped on the shoulder from behind. I turned around to see a tall bulky man with a flat top. He was wearing sunglasses and a "Muscle Beach" tee shirt. The shirt was pulled tight against monstrous shoulders and biceps, and his neck appeared to be thicker than his head.

"Are you the guy who took money from my wife?" He did not appear to be asking the question with the intent of piling more upon his spouse's charitable contribution. In fact, he seemed angry. I couldn't lie. The woman was standing right there, a little behind him on his left side.

"Yes I am. Thank you so much, I really needed it. She's a lifesaver and you're a lucky man." I smiled broadly as I said this. I was inviting him to take part in the joy of his wife's giving. He declined the invitation.

"What did you need the money for?"

"To get my car out of the impound lot."

He looked at his wife and she nodded. She said nothing, apparently cowed into silence by her husband. I felt bad for putting her in this awkward situation.

"Where is this impound lot?"

"Right here in San Francisco."

"What's the address?"

"200 McAllister Street," I replied. I don't know what you might find if you go to 200 McAllister Street, but if it's an impound lot then that is a huge coincidence.

"What's your name?"

"James Bauer."

"And where are you from?"

"Reno."

"Can I see your I.D.?"

"I wish you could, but it was in my wallet, which was stolen. That's the whole problem." I would be lying if I said that I made my reply to his question with the steady calm of a seasoned criminal, and I will admit that I was terribly frightened of the large angry man who stood before me. Everything about him, from the tone of his voice to his physical posture, carried with it the threat of violence, and, due to the vast disparity in size between us, there could be no doubt that if it came to a physical confrontation I would be the loser.

"Kind of convenient isn't it, the way your wallet just disappeared?"

"I don't think so. I'd say it's very inconvenient! I need it to get my car!" I had intended to speak with the hot-tempered tones of the wrongly accused but was betrayed by an ugly quaver of the vocal mechanism.

"Uh-huh," he sneered.

I decided it was time to turn up the moral indignation, "I hope you're not implying that I was lying about the whole thing, that I was trying to run some kind of pathetic con on your charitable wife!" The quaver was still there, betraying me!

"That's exactly what I'm implying."

"Well look" I said, pained that anyone could think me dishonest, "if it's going to be a big deal, I'll give you back the money." Apparently, this was the wrong thing to say, because it seemed to trigger a very negative reaction in the flat-topped monster confronting me.

"Oh, you will, will you?" His sneer curled around the edges and took on an even more sinister appearance.

"Yes!" I began to rummage about the various pockets of my suit but couldn't remember which one I had stuffed the

210

wad of money into. I thought that if I found it quickly enough, I might avoid a beating. I could feel the money burning me, and I had to get rid of it, but my suit had *too many pockets*, and my search was fruitless.

"You take advantage of *my* wife, you steal *my* money, and you think you can just give it back and everything's all better? Is that it? Is that what you think?"

I was terrified and my voice failed me for a moment. When I finally found it again my words rang hollow and seemed completely void of argumentative weight, "Hey, I didn't steal anything, I really needed it to get my car I . . ." My explanation was cut short by a right hook that caught me on my left cheekbone and sent me sprawling across the pavement.

The angry flat top man rubbed his right hand to relieve the residual sting caused by its contact with my face and yelled, "Get up! Get up!"

I was groggy and my head was spinning. The last thing I wanted to do was get up. The concrete sidewalk was the most comfortable surface in the world at that moment. If I stood, he would hit me again, of that I was sure. What would he do, I wondered, if I stayed on the ground? This question was soon answered as he grabbed me by the lapels of my twenty-five-dollar suit and lifted me off the sidewalk. He looked at me, our faces four inches apart, as my feet hovered six inches off the ground. His breath reeked of crab cakes, veins the size of garden hoses bulged out on his forehead, and his eyes were red with beer and fury. "You get up when I tell you to get up!"

"Yes sir," I mumbled feebly. There was a circle of people around us watching impassively. They seemed to think that they were witnessing a piece of less amusing than average street theater. No one lifted a finger to help, no one ran to get the police, no one even raised a soothing voice

211

against the violent thug who was holding a dark suited man by the lapels and shouting angrily in his face.

Doesn't a suit count for anything these days?

He set my feet back down on the pavement and then punched me in the stomach. My body doubled over at a ninety-degree angle as it began to sail through the air before landing, buttocks first, on the pavement once again. I toppled over onto my back, striking my head on the hard ground as I did so. My whole body ached from the effects of the two punches and the two violent collisions with the sidewalk. The tall muscular man looked down at my bruised frame a moment before bending towards me. I was afraid that he was going to hit me again and I flinched. He smiled but didn't hit me again. Instead, he opened my coat and pulled the wad of cash from the inside breast pocket. *So that's where it had been!* He didn't limit himself to the seventy dollars I had scammed from his wife. He took every last dollar I had before he walked off with my former benefactor.

I lay motionless for a moment and stared up at the overcast sky. Finally, a man from the crowd that had surrounded the scene crouched by my side. "Are you okay?" he asked.

I knew I would survive my wounds, so I answered in the affirmative.

"Do you want me to get the police?"

"Naw, I had it coming I guess," I said as I sat up. I could hear the "*lub dub, lub dub*" throb of my heart in my ears. Each beat stabbed my head like a shard of sharp glass.

"Are you sure you're ok? You took a couple good hits."

"Yeah, I'm fine," I lied "I'll be alright. I just need to sit down for a few minutes and collect myself."

He helped me to a nearby bench and I sat on it. After assuring himself that I was not going to die, he left my side and returned to whatever it was he had been doing before his pleasant day had been interrupted by an unpleasant scene of violence. I sat on the bench for a while, collecting my strength and gathering the shards of my scattered mind, before standing, and, like Napoleon after Moscow, wandering away from the scene of the disaster.

That was it. The research portion of writing my novel was over. I was on my way home. I didn't have enough money for bus fair, let alone a cab, so I had to walk a few hilly San Francisco miles to get back to my home.

I slid they key into the lock of my building's front door and turned it. The oiled mettle clicked, the door swung wide and I was pushed through the doorway by the hasty March breeze. The elevator stood open and I walked inside, punching the button for the fourth floor with my knuckles. The box rose quickly above street level and within a few seconds I stood in the hall before my apartment door. I was home at last.

I stepped into my apartment and sat on the plush couch. My aching body sank deep into the cool cushions and I knew that I would die happy if I passed away in the leathery embrace of that comfortable sofa. I had felt nothing so soft in weeks. The apartment was dark, the blinds were drawn, and the noises of the street sounded muffled and distant. I was separated from the brutal urban outdoors by bricks and mortar, drywall and double paned glass. I was home. There was nothing to be done but take a long shower, and then fall asleep in the hope that I would dream of Abby.

Chapter 35

Everything about being home was great. Eating hot food brought to me by (lavishly tipped) delivery guys was great. Being clean and smelling of soap and shampoo was great. Sleeping in a bed that swallowed me with its infinite softness was great. Being warm and dry all the time was great. Feeling safe behind locked doors was great. Everything was great, great, great.

Except for two things. Two things were not great.

The first of these things was the next step I had to take with Abby. For the past few weeks Abby had been a sort of dream most of the time (except, of course, for the day when I had actually seen her). Dreams are great because they don't require anything from us. We can just sit there and enjoy mentally floating around in some lovely and unlikely future while muttering "someday." And that's what I had been doing with Abby. Because while I was homeless I was not in a position to do anything about winning her, I could just enjoy thinking about her, trying to convince myself that she would be mine one day, and then imagining how great that would be when it happened.

Now, however, I was in a position where I could do something about Abby. I was no longer living on the street, I was no longer wrapped up with that terrible private investigator, and I had taken a shower and shaved off my greasy beard. Dreaming is fine when you aren't in a position to do anything about achieving your dream, but once it's possible to take some steps in the right direction you'd better start taking those steps or that dream will be revealed as hollow. I had reached that stage where I couldn't just dream anymore; I would now have to do something.

The problem was that I wasn't sure exactly what I should do. Unless things had changed, she still had a boyfriend. If she was still wrapped up with Chad I would have to move cautiously, getting myself into an apparently harmless position of friendship, while working subtly to undermine the other guy. I had never had to sabotage, undermine, or backstab anybody, but I was ready to do whatever it took to bring him down.

If they had already broken up, which was possible, then I could give into my instinct to behave rashly. I have always acted with conservatism, with caution, with a wooden refusal to move forward at all, really. But there was something in Abigail that made me want to rush stupidly forward, to be reckless, to be foolish, to make a spectacle of myself. If Abigail didn't have a boyfriend, I didn't think I could trust myself to spend much time with her before blurting out the "L" word.

"Love" is a surprisingly difficult word to say. Supposedly we all want to be loved, but to hear the wrong person say "I love you" at the wrong time is a repellent thing. Such a declaration is an embarrassment for the loved person and a source of humiliation for the declarer. We are supposed to hide our love and wait for the person we love to show a hint through a chink in their emotional armor before we stab them with "love." But I could feel the phrase "I love you" burning inside me, and I knew that it was going to burn hotter and hotter the more time I spent with Abby, and I would be forced to let it out at some point or it would burn me alive.

It seemed to me that the thing to do was to give Abby a copy of my novel. I had told her that I would let her read it as soon as I had a draft, and she had expressed enthusiasm. Giving her my book and then meeting with her to discuss it would be perfectly aboveboard even if she still had a boyfriend. And if I met with her and discovered that she didn't (and she had let slip a few things the last time I had met her at Hunan Burrito that made me think that the charms of Chadwick Blowington were beginning to fade for her) then I was probably going to just tell her "I LOVE YOU," as loudly and inappropriately as possible, even though I knew that this was a bad idea.

The second thing that wasn't great was tied to the first. I had to actually write a novel. I don't know if you know this about writing novels (you probably do, since you have the novel writing disease the same as everyone else and have been working on one for the past five years) but it is a difficult business. James Joyce averaged fewer than 80 words a day over his career. At that rate I would finish in a decade. I would have to write at a Stephen King kind of pace.

I began writing in every spare moment for two weeks straight, and during that two week period I wrote everything you have just read, right up to this sentence. That's about 4,700 words per day. If speed is what makes an author great, then I just crushed and humiliated James Joyce, and almost everybody else.

I was motivated by the fact that I wouldn't have a pretext to get in touch with Abby until I had finished. Now the pretext is complete (well, complete enough) and I'm going to send this manuscript to Abby tomorrow morning. I guess I'm going to do the rash, foolish, stupid thing after all. My novel isn't quite finished yet, but I think you'll agree that what I've written will give her a lot to think about.

Chapter 36

For two days I heard nothing from Abigail. You can imagine how I felt as those awful 48 hours ground by. It is tough to give your manuscript to somebody you respect, knowing that you are giving them a sort of homework assignment, asking them to spend hours reading your book instead of doing all the better things they could be doing, knowing that you are offering a glimpse at what they may well regard as a failure, and knowing that you have exposed your ugly little self in a million little ways.

Exposing yourself through your writing is something that a writer feels he is doing even when he has written something bizarre, otherworldly, or experimental. You can't help but leave pieces of yourself in every character, in every setting, and in every piece of dialogue. But what I had written wasn't some way out there experimental thing. It was very close to autobiography and the veneer of fiction was extremely thin. I changed Abigail's name, and a few other little details, but that wouldn't protect me.

Right after I emailed it to Abby, I opened up my copy on Google Docs and began to read it over. When I had pushed "send" only one minute before, my book had looked pretty good. In fact, it had looked great. Not only was it going to be published, I thought, it would probably be a bestseller, and there could be no doubt that the critics would praise it. It would likely end up as a beloved classic, but I was humble enough to acknowledge that this would ultimately be for posterity to decide. Now however, precisely 63 seconds after I had sent it off to Abby, it inexplicably became a grotesque embarrassment. Why were all my sentences so clunky and inelegant? Why did I always seem to use the *mot injuste?* Why did I tell that story about that time I had nearly crapped my pants? Why didn't the plot have any drive to it?

Why were all the characters so poorly drawn? Why was the action so flat and uninteresting? Why did the dialogue sound so fake? And where did all these typos come from? There were four on the first page alone, and they had not been there 63 seconds ago.

Of course, none of that was the worst of it. Not even close. Having sent Abby a literary abomination wasn't nearly as painful as having sent her a sort of misguided love letter. As I had written that paragraph about being particularly attracted to Asian women, I had been thinking, "This isn't good. Abby is going to read this. This is creepy and I should delete it." I did not delete it. I left it in because somehow it felt like it had to be part of the book.

As I was writing all that guff about falling in love at first sight, I had thought, "You know what? This is a bad idea. Abby is going to read this. Do you really want to tell her that you fell in love with her at first sight? She might not even like you. How about you wait until you're engaged and then tell her? You have literally only seen her two times. This is a bad idea. You should delete it." It remained undeleted when I sent my book to Abby.

All that stuff about the phrase "I love you" burning inside of me? You've seen it. You know I left it in.

I could feel my face reddening and my heart hammering and my brain sloshing around in my skull. People tell you to "put your heart out there" and to "take risks for love," but as I clearly stated way back in Chapter 2, I have never been a gambling man. I have never put myself out there. That was the sort of the key to my whole character, but Abby had smashed that version of me. I'd done all sorts of ridiculous things since I met her, though none of them was half as foolish as sending her a manuscript that was all about how much I loved her and the lengths to which I would go to get her.

218

I couldn't look at my computer screen anymore and I slid out of my chair as if my bones had been teleported away while the rest of me was left behind. I lay in a puddle on the floor, thinking dark thoughts and hating my stupid book.

After those 48 hours passed, I received a text. I would have preferred a call, but I'd take what I could get. She said that she had read my book and that she had some "comments." She said we should meet for lunch, but not at Hunan Burrito. We arranged a date. Or a meeting. Whatever. We were going to eat lunch together and she was going to make some "comments" on my book.

This text exchange occurred on a Friday evening, so I had sixteen additional hours to agonize. I looked at my book again, and then looked away in horror moments later. I got back into my puddle position on the ground and moaned. I dreaded the comments that were coming my way.

I did not sleep well that night. My soft bed worked none of its magic. I tossed and I turned and somehow suffered nightmares without ever actually sleeping. I got out of bed at about eight o'clock and wandered around my apartment. Bedroom, kitchen, living room, bathroom, that's all there is too it. Not much room for pacing, but somehow I managed to pace miles. At 12:37 I put on my coat and walked out of my apartment. I was on my way to see Abby for the third time.

We were meeting in a small Italian restaurant on Fillmore. As soon as I walked in I was hit with a warm wave of delicious Italian smells, but it didn't awaken my appetite. Abby was already seated when I got there, looking as stunning as ever with her bright eyes shining inside the frames of her glasses, her long black hair shimmering like a night sky filled with stars, every inch of her perfect and unimprovable. "I read your book," she said with an inscrutable tone as I sat down across from her at a table so tiny I doubted it could hold plates for two people.

"Ah, is that so?" I asked as I reddened.

"Before we talk about it, I think you should read something I wrote."

"That sounds fair." I was glad to have the reprieve.

She handed me fifteen double spaced sheets of paper. The words were written in Times New Roman, 12-point font. I said, "We've never actually talked about your novel, have we?"

"No. All I have is this chapter. I don't think it will bore you."

"I'm sure it won't."

Chapter 1

I'd had plans to meet Chad for lunch, but ever since his collection of stories had been published he'd been acting like an asshole. Being late for everything all the time was the way he showed people that he was more important than they were. But I've seen the letters from his publisher, and I know how many copies *Neptune's Nipples* has sold. But even if he'd sold millions it would be no excuse for being such a jerk.

But he was my man, so instead of fighting with him every time he showed up late, I just planned around it. If you can get a guy to be less selfish and to change for the better, great. If you can't get him to change (and you probably can't) then you have two options: you can either dump him or figure out how to make peace with all the things he does that annoy you. I had already realized that Chad wasn't going to change and now I was at the point where I had to either accept the way he was or dump him. I wanted to dump him, and probably would have already if he wasn't such a smooth talker. He had a superhuman ability to piss people off and then talk them out of their anger. If he could teach this skill, he'd be a millionaire. Chad could be charming and amusing too, although every day he seemed to be getting less and less so as his arrogance took over. He was becoming unbearable.

Because I knew that he would be late, I came prepared with a book. I had asked him to meet me at a Mexican restaurant a few blocks away from my office. It was an unpopular place that would probably be half empty. The restaurant would be nice and quiet, and I could read there in peace. It was a perfect place for a woman and her reading material.

When I got there, it was more than half empty. There were ten tables in the dining room, and only one was occupied. This one table was being used by a guy reading a thick hardback. It looked like he had managed to spill sauce on it already. I was tempted to give him a sharp little lecture about taking better care of his books, especially if the book he was reading was a library book, but I decided not to. If I tried to straighten out every man I ran into who was doing something thoughtless I'd never do anything else. Without taking his eyes from the words on the page in front of him, he wiped the sauce away with a napkin, mostly just smearing it. I cringed.

The waitress brought me to a table directly across from that lone man and I sat facing his direction because I always like to have my back against the wall so nobody can take me by surprise. He was still engrossed in his book, but now that I was seated I could see his face a little better. He was kind of cute, for a defacer of books at least. He had a kind looking face, he was clean shaven, and he had brown hair that matched his brown eyes. He was dressed in a suit. I've always liked a man in a suit. It was black and somehow managed to straddle the line between conservative and trendy. I caught this in a moment and then I turned my attention to the menu. I sensed him finally look up at me while I was looking down at the specials. There were just the two of us, seated awkwardly so that we had to face one another, and it was natural that each of us would take a peek at the other. I didn't think anything of it.

After I had ordered I pulled a paperback copy of *The Code of the Woosters* out of my bag. *The Code of the Woosters* is my favorite novel and I was immediately wrapped up in it. It's one of the Jeeves and Wooster books, about a rich and idle dimwit named Bertie Wooster and his genius of a gentleman's gentleman, Jeeves. Jeeves is not a

222

butler, by the way; he's a valet. Pronounced with the full "t" sound at the end. Not that it matters.

I was soon smiling and laughing along with the text. Wodehouse has a gift for giving nearly every sentence a somehow comic inflection, at once beautiful and amusing. Then he piles on an abundance of eccentric characters: Gussie Fink-Nottle, the spectacle wearing newt-fancier, Madeline Bassett, the cotton-headed baby talker who thinks that bunnies are gnomes in attendance on the Fairy Queen and that the stars are God's daisy chain, Sir Roderick Spode, a comic incarnation of Oswald Mosley who aspires to be a dictator and wants to beat Bertie to a jelly. As soon as I started reading everything else vanished. The stranger across from me, the Mexican restaurant, the entire city of San Francisco; all of it disappeared. I was in Wodehouse's idealized vision of Edwardian England. It is a lovely place to visit.

Then I heard a voice, "You seem to be enjoying that novel."

Oh no, I thought, he may be good looking, but that guy is a Nattering Nitwit. "Nattering Nitwit" is the term I coined to describe people who try to talk to you when you are reading and would clearly rather be left alone. How could this guy think that I would prefer talking to him to reading P.G. Wodehouse? What arrogance! His behavior was as Modern Dutch at Sir Watkyn Bassett's cow creamer. I decided to be polite and then to get back to my book as soon as possible.

"I love it." I said, "This is my third time reading it. It's so funny."

"I love it too," he said. And I almost rolled my eyes. Oh sure, pretend to be into what I'm into; it's the oldest and lamest trick in the book. What kind of dumb shit did he take me for? At the very least, guys, please have the decency to

223

be yourselves. "All the Jeeves books are great, but *The Code of the Woosters* is my favorite. Sir Roderick Spode, Gussy Fink-Nottle, Stinker Pinker, Madeline Bassett, the whole crew, really. It's pretty much perfect."

Oh, I realized, *it's not a trick*. This guy has actually read *The Code of the Woosters*. Who would have guessed that name dropping "Gussy Fink-Nottle" would actually work with a girl? I realized I sorta liked this guy. Nobody who is into Wodehouse can be all bad, so I smiled and said, "Yes, it's not Modern Dutch at all."

I had made a stupid jokey reference to *The Code of the Woosters*, and this guy laughed like it was the greatest thing he had ever heard. I think it was then that I sorta started to like him. There was a warmth in his eyes as he laughed that radiated right into me. I don't believe in love at first sight. It's a ridiculous idea, but the fact that we could both understand and laugh at my Modern Dutch reference... I don't know. It kind of felt like a connection.

Books are bridges. And even though I had just met this guy, and still didn't even know his name, our love of *The Code of the Woosters* had linked us in a weird way. At that moment what I wanted to do was freeze time, find this guy's house, look at his bookcases and then come back to finish the conversation. You can tell a lot about a guy from the books he reads. I've had an idea in my head for a dating app where each person inputs all the books they've read in the past five years and the app matches them up. I think it would work.

I could tell the guy liked me, but I hoped he wasn't one of those white guy creepers who are into Asian women. "I'm sorry I interrupted your reading," he said, but I could tell this wasn't true. He wasn't sorry at all. Still, I liked the apology. It showed that he knew that what he had done was outside of the acceptable in normal circumstances.

224

"Oh that's ok," I said, and I was a little surprised to realize that I meant it, "I'm always glad to be interrupted by anyone who loves Wodehouse like I do."

"You can't be unhappy when reading one of the Jeeves books."

"Oh, I agree. Have you read any of his other novels?"

"Yeah. He wrote almost a hundred of them."

"It has always seemed strange to me that someone who wrote so much about lazy 'gentlemen of leisure' could actually have such a strong work ethic."

As we talked my intuition that he was into me only increased. He had that nervousness that a guy gets when he meets a girl that he's really attracted to. When a guy acts that way around me I can either be annoyed or flattered, depending on whether I like him. I was flattered.

"By the way," he said, "My name is Daniel."

I told him my name and we continued chatting. He told me about his job, and I must admit it didn't sound very interesting. If I'm being honest, it was boring as hell. I was doing my best to look engaged, but he clearly realized he was talking too much about himself and he decided to get me talking.

After some spluttering, he asked me, "What's your novel about?"

I groaned inside. Here we were, just a couple of people having a conversation about books and he has to ruin it by asking that tired question. I can't blame him; it's the question that people seem to ask these days. But I had a dirty secret; I didn't have a novel. And I had no intention of ever writing a novel. I loved books, but I realized early on that my love was the love of a reader, not a writer. I flipped it around and said, "I'd rather hear you talk about yours. What's your novel about?"

In my experience, guys love it when you ask them about their novels. It gratifies their vanity. "Ah, this girl wants to hear about my novel because this girl wants ME," they seem to say to themselves. For exactly that reason it's a question that I usually avoid asking. But Daniel's vanity didn't seem to have been at all pumped up by the question. Instead he looked almost scared. "What's my novel about?" he asked, clearly stalling.

"Yeah. What's it about?"

He was quiet for a moment, his eyes darting around the room, before he shouted, "THE HOMELESS!"

"What about them?"

"How much they suffer," he said. There was a pause and I watched his brain madly scramble for something more to say until suddenly he shouted, "I'M GOING TO LIVE ON THE STREET FOR A MONTH. FOR RESEARCH!"

It was a little weird, to tell you the truth. I could tell he didn't want to talk about his novel any more than I wanted to talk about my non-novel, so I brought it back to other people's books, "Research? Like George Orwell spending time as a tramp?"

Then we talked about Orwell for a while. I was really clicking with him and I could tell he was going to ask me for my phone number at any moment, and I had decided that I'd give it to him. It would be Chad's own fault for being so late. But then, suddenly, Chad was there.

"Why are we eating at this shitty place?" he asked. My heart sank. You heart isn't supposed to sink when you see your boyfriend, is it?

"It's quiet." I told him, "You're always late these days and I wanted to be someplace quiet where I could read while I waited."

I almost laughed when I glanced at Daniel's face. He was so sad. I mean, I liked him, and I know that laughing is

226

the wrong reaction, but you should have seen how comically hangdog his face was. I had known that Chad was a menace looming on the horizon, but from Daniel's perspective he was a terrible surprise. "This Daniel. He noticed I was reading *The Code of the Woosters* and we have been talking about how it's one of our favorite books."

"I haven't read it," Chad said as he sat down, "I only like serious literature."

There's a moment in romantic comedies when the girl's boyfriend does something so awful, so tasteless, so rude, so stupid, or so selfish that you see her suddenly realize, "Wait, I don't want to be with this guy. This guy is a piece of shit." I had just had that moment. Only a monster could think he is too good for P.G. Wodehouse.

Daniel, to his credit, didn't retreat from the table as soon as Chad showed up. It was awkward, but he tried to make the best of things. I think he was trying to just keep the game going in the hope that he could somehow winkle away my phone number. He pointed to Chad's collection of short stories (Chad carried them around everywhere he went) and said, "Well, that looks like some serious literature. Is it any good?"

"Very serious. I wrote it."

"Chad publi…" I started to say before Chad cut me off.

"Chadwick! Please, Abigail, I go by Chadwick now!"

And that was another one of those, "Wait, I don't want to be with this guy because he totally sucks" moments. I'd had two in a thirty second period. That had to be a record. What I should have done is break up with him on the spot. Instead I said, "Chadwick published his first collection of short stories a month ago."

I sort of expected Daniel to flee at this point, but again, he didn't, instead he said, "Are you working on anything now?"

227

Chad had taken an instant dislike to Daniel, which is understandable. If a man shows up at a restaurant to eat lunch with his girlfriend and finds her being chatted up by some rando, he's going to dislike the rando. It's a given. Daniel could tell this, but he was still clinging on. To stay at the table with Chad he was willing to hear about Chad's novel. He was about to hear about the billions and billions of years that led up to the pinnacle of evolution: Chad. His willingness to listen to this showed that not only did Daniel have a thing for me, he was willing to suffer for me.

Daniel sat there and took it like a champ as Chad spun his tale for fifteen minutes. I liked how even though he clearly didn't like Chad, he tried to look like he was interested. He made a real effort. His face mechanically moved through the motions of expressing interest, respect, and even wonder. Chad, blinded by his vanity, took all these expressions at face value, and as his due.

Once Chad finished telling his story I could see Daniel looking for an excuse somehow stay talking with us, but he didn't find one and he had to go. As I watched him slide his book into a courier bag and slump out of the restaurant, I wanted to go with him. I also noticed he had a nice ass.

I said earlier that I didn't believe in love at first sight, and this is true. You can't fall in love with somebody at first glance. But I had just discovered that you can call in love in 25 minutes, which is still a shockingly short period of time if you think about it.

Chapter 37

I have read a lot of books. I've read *The Code of the Woosters*, *Hamlet, Don Quixote, A Farewell to Arms*, and *A Handful of Dust*. I've read every single novel ever written by Charles Dickens. I've read The Bible, The Koran, the Tao Te Ching, and the Bhagavad Gita. I've read *the Chronicles of Narnia*. I've read *A Tree Grows in Brooklyn*. I've read the *Lord of the Rings* trilogy and the *USA* trilogy. I've read every one of Guy de Maupassant's stories. I've read HP Lovecraft and Stephen King. I've read *Green Eggs and Ham*. I've read every Harry Bosch mystery. Twice. The same goes for the Philip Marlowe novels. I've read *The Decline and Fall of the Roman Empire*. I've read the *Dune* series, the *Expanse* series, and the *Foundation* series. I've read the first page of *Finnegan's Wake* six times (and the second page zero times). I've read Proust, Tolstoy, Wharton, Austen, Eliot, Hugo, and Flannery O'Connor. I've read Roth, Murakami, and Vargas Llosa. I've read about fifty westerns by Louis L'Amour. And in all those millions of words I'd never found anything half as good as the fifteen pages Abby had written.

I told her so.

"I liked your book too," she said.

"I think we have a novel. Together. Without your chapter I don't have a story at all."

"I agree. We should shuffle our pages together."

"You weren't creeped out by the fact that I, or, the character in my book, is particularly attracted to Asian women?"

"I'll make an exception in your case, and his."

"The bit where I hired a private detective to find you… that didn't bother you?"

She paused, "Did that really happen? He really got murdered?"

I nodded my head.

"Wow. I thought maybe you put that in there as a sort of dramatic embellishment."

I shook my head.

"You've been through a lot."

"I know."

"And you did it for me."

"Yeah."

"You're lucky I like you too. Otherwise your novel would be…"

"Humiliating. I know. I love you, by the way."

"I know; I read your book. So, what now?"

"I think we kiss. That's the sort of thing that happens at the end of a love story."

We leaned towards each other, fortunate that the table between us was so small, and our lips met. The waiter chose that moment to show up with my ravioli and Abby's chicken parmesan, but we ignored him. He stood there for at least a minute, doubtless feeling very awkward as our food cooled in his hands. But we didn't even notice him.

Chapter 38

One final thing before I finish. I think it is important for you to know that I am a robot. Abby is also a robot. In fact, everyone in this book is a robot. Chadwick, Glen, Proctor, Carlos, the Knifeman, Sandra: all robots.

Printed in Poland
by Amazon Fulfillment
Poland Sp. z o.o., Wrocław